'For the pas[t] ... tried to tune ... except in a s... way.'

'Why?' Gerard said bluntly.

'Oh…' Jan hesitated. 'Let me just say that I had a clash between the very personal and the professional…'

'Hmm…' he murmured. 'I think I know what you mean. Sounds like a variation on a fairly common theme.'

Jan bit her lip, keeping her eyes focused on the floor, willing the color in her cheeks to subside. Now why the hell did I tell him that? she admonished herself.

Rebecca Lang trained to be a State Registered Nurse in Kent, England, where she was born. Her main focus of interest became operating theatre work, and she gained extensive experience in all types of surgery on both sides of the Atlantic. Now living in Toronto, Canada, she is married to a Canadian pathologist, and has three children. When not writing, Rebecca enjoys gardening, reading, theatre, exploring new places, and anything to do with the study of people.

LET TOMORROW COME

BY
REBECCA LANG

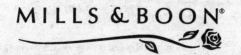

First published in Great Britain 1999
Harlequin Mills & Boon Limited,
Eton House, 18-24 Paradise Road, Richmond, Surrey TW9 1SR

© Rebecca Lang 1999

ISBN 0 263 81283 9

Set in Times Roman 10 on 11½ pt.
03-9901-55815-D

Printed and bound in Norway
by AIT Trondheim AS, Trondheim

CHAPTER ONE

'STOP'

The command scarcely registered on Jan Newsome as she wrestled with the minibus on the pot-holed road, going much too fast as it entered the outskirts of the banana plantation.

The muscles of her arms ached from the effort of keeping the unfamiliar vehicle on the winding road that had, for the last few miles or so, gone steadily uphill and was only now showing signs of leveling out a little.

The rain forest, with its dense, luxuriant green foliage, was gradually giving way to scattered patches of cultivation, the beginning of the familiar banana groves that grew right up to the roadside. She had increased speed accordingly.

Along the way from the town, miles back, she had seen small groups of men here and there, clearing debris off the road. No one had paid much attention to her, only looking up to stare briefly as she drove past in the eight-seater mini-van, the only vehicle she had been able to hire in a hurry after her arrival on the island to take her and her luggage to Manara.

Only by keeping her eyes firmly on the road was she able to prevent the van from veering off into a ditch or plunging down one of the many steep, wooded inclines beyond the narrow verge. It would take her a while, too, to get used to driving on the left again and using a vehicle with a gear shift.

For what must have been the hundredth time since her arrival, she found herself speculating on how much had deteriorated since her last visit two years previously, especially this road, the only major paved road on the island, which ran from the airport in the south to the north part of the island by many devious detours.

Perhaps she had looked at everything through rose-colored glasses, she thought soberly. This time things were different. For another thing, she was more mature. She had been in love then...with John. That certainly made a difference. These days she never whispered his name to herself as she had then, missing him.

Jan found herself smiling wryly as she thought about him briefly. Her surroundings now gave all that a dream-like quality. There had been other men in her life since John, although none she had been in love with. She tried to block him out of her mind altogether, and was mostly successful at it these days. That was all part of an emotional barrier she had put up. Since John there had been safety in numbers.

Who had shouted at her to stop she had no idea, not daring to take her eyes off their fixed point on the road ahead—if they had been shouting at her at all. She saw no reason to stop. Her weary mind was mostly occupied with thoughts and vivid images of her father who, at that very moment, might be lying ill at Manara. Anything could have happened in the few days since all useful communication had been cut off by bad weather.

Since Jan had received the telephone call for help from her father, her life had changed drastically. In a matter of hours she had taken leave of absence from her job in Boston—something in itself that caused her anxiety as it was a new job for which there had been fierce competition in the first place—and booked a flight to St Bonar.

She had also managed, by telephoning people she knew in the medical profession on the island, to arrange for a possible job for herself...or she thought she had. There had been no time to confirm anything because the weather had intervened, with storms and heavy rain. Her father's doctor on the island, Don McLean, had not known her father was ill when she had got through to him. That had been during a brief contact before the storm. He had promised to find out.

That was typical of her father—not to ask for help from anyone except family, and then from her because she was closer and because she was a doctor. Denial that he needed help was part of his personality. He had made her promise not to contact her mother in England—not yet. So far she had complied with his wishes, but only because her mother was fully occupied, nursing her own mother.

'"The best laid plans of mice and men…"' Jan muttered resignedly to herself as she blew a strand of errant hair out of her mouth, her face buffeted by a welcome breeze from the open window of the van. There was no way that she could exist for long without earning money. And it was not often that her father admitted he was not feeling well so when he did she knew that things were serious. One good thing, she had at least finished all her training. If she lost her job, so be it…

A tight knot of apprehension had lodged itself somewhere in the region of her stomach since that telephone call and had refused to go away. Maybe, just maybe, it was time to give up the house and land on this island—even though the very thought of doing that made every nerve in her body cry out a protest. Her grandfather had arranged things so that the place could be theirs in perpetuity. That had been his hope and ambition. It would be a defeat after all these years. And yet… The past was the past after all.

A reflection of movement in the side mirror induced her to slow down. Against the glare of sunlight she squinted at that reflection as it grew nearer. Coming towards her from the rear, along the narrow grass shoulder of the road, was a man on horseback. He was moving fast, apparently waving for her to pull over. Jan yanked at the gear shift and eased the van to one side, as far off the road as she could in the narrow space, and switched off the engine.

Taking off her sunglasses, she swivelled round in her seat to watch the man approach, then stop and dismount a short distance away. The horse was a big chestnut-colored mare, lathered with sweat. In the sudden quiet Jan could hear birds, chirping, in a dense forested area that separated banana fields just beyond the open window of the van.

Leaving his horse to eat grass, the man walked towards her. There was a deliberation about his movements, an air of lazy authority, that made Jan tense. He had something of the same stance that police had in the city when they had pulled you over to give you a speeding ticket. He was tall, heavy-looking and muscular. At one time, a few years ago, she would have known practically everyone of European descent on the island who was not a transient, there being relatively few of them. This man, she considered speculatively, she had never seen before.

Through a haze of heat Jan watched his long legs moving rhythmically as he swung his body with an unconscious masculine grace. In those few moments Jan was surprised that she could admire him in an oddly detached sort of way, as though she were watching a tableau in which she herself was not taking part. Maybe that was what extreme tiredness did to you.

He came up slowly to the open window of the van and planted his folded arms on the edge. It seemed to her several minutes before he spoke. 'Where the hell are you going? Didn't you hear me shout at you to stop?' he said.

The accent was curious: slightly American, Jan decided, with some British overtones and a certain deep timbre of the West Indies—that slow, caressing lilt that she usually found attractive.

Involuntarily Jan drew back from his closeness and shifted herself a few inches along the seat, not understanding why she did so. The movement was not lost on him, and his mouth curved in a slight, brief, sardonic quirk as he gave her a slow, assessing stare.

He was younger than she had first thought, in spite of a tanned and somewhat weathered look. His proximity forced her to stare at him full on. His features were strong and hard, with a classic straight nose above a very masculine mouth that showed no hint of a welcoming smile.

What she registered immediately was that he looked exhausted. The whites of his eyes were bloodshot and he had that fatigued look that came from having had too little sleep over a long time—a feeling that she knew so well. As she appraised him in those few moments he was very obviously doing the same to her with shrewd brown eyes.

It had been a long time since she had felt as aware of a man, and the feeling came as a surprise. The necessities of her profession served to squash any youthful vestiges of self-consciousness and coyness in her dealings with men, the process dating from the time she had entered medical school. Yet now she felt a tingling heat, invading her body, that had little to do with the oven-like temperature inside the van which was in full sun.

At the same time Jan became aware of how washed-out and dishevelled she must look, her face without make-up, her skin without color from a hard winter spent in Boston, where she had been finishing up what could only be described as a punishing post-graduate course in surgery, before starting her new job.

Her fair hair, almost shoulder length, had been whipped by the wind to something resembling a tangled bird's nest. Wispy bits of it fanned her cheeks. The thin, sleeveless blouse that she wore was plastered to her body with sweat. Such a contrast she must seem, she reflected ruefully, to everything else on this exotic, colorful island where people and things appeared larger than life...including him. It wasn't surprising that he was staring at her.

'I did hear a shout,' she admitted, 'but I didn't realize you were shouting at me.'

'Since yours was the only vehicle on the road, I think you could have figured it out...and saved me the time I've wasted, chasing after you.' There was an edge of sarcasm to his voice as he continued to look at her, and a tenseness about him now that bespoke, Jan guessed, extreme exhaustion. Compassion for his state came readily to her as she could see something of the storm damage that surrounded them.

She noticed the fine sheen of sweat on his face as he moved closer to her, his head and shoulders inside the van, out of the sun's glare, as though to emphasize his effort in galloping after her. To express his exasperation further, he ran a hand through his thick, dark hair.

'I was concentrating on driving,' she retorted. 'I'm sorry. I'm not used to this sort of vehicle. Why do you want me to stop? There were no signs on the road.'

'There's been a landslide up ahead, completely blocking the road. The road crews haven't got up that far yet to do anything about it. There's also been an accident back there, where I was when you went by—a mud-slide, a few people injured. That's been dealt with, but the roads are not safe for you to be bombing along the way you were. They've been undermined by heavy rain.'

'I see. Yes, I should have thought about that,' she said, and broke eye contact with him, finding his concentrated regard oddly unnerving. 'Damn!' she added softly, gazing ahead up the road to where it very soon disappeared around a bend.

Up ahead, dense, tangled foliage, interspersed with brilliantly colored flowers, grew down an incline to the very edge of the hard surface of the road on one side. The still, hot air around them was full of the scent of moist vegetation. 'I'm sorry,' she said again. 'I guess I should have stopped. I am in a bit of a hurry.'

'You do know, I presume, there's been a minor hurricane here—not just a bit of rain?' he said. ' If one can call such a thing minor.' The sarcasm was a little heavier now, though nonetheless subtle. Jan was used to picking up nuances from the male sex—it came with the territory of working mostly with male colleagues.

He did not seem to be a man who liked women much. The thought came to Jan at the same moment as the feeling of dismay at his news about the landslide, even though his eyes were going over her in a way that belied such an observation.

Her mind ranged quickly over possible alternatives to this route. None came immediately to mind. She was bone weary. It was her turn now to run a hand distractedly through her mess of hair, pushing it back from her heated face. She moistened her dry lips with her tongue, feeling desperately thirsty.

'Yes, I know there's been a bad storm,' she said.

'Then you'll know how much rain can fall here in a matter of minutes...what damage it can do.'

Jan nodded. 'I've been holed up in Barbados for two days, waiting for a flight here. It wasn't exactly something I was expecting as this isn't the hurricane season,' she said calmly, masking her dismay—hoping he would realize that she was no greenhorn in this part of the world. 'Do you know how long it will be before it gets cleared...the landslide?'

She looked at him speculatively. Perhaps he was some sort of visiting engineer, temporarily on the island to work on a project. 'Twelve-month wonders' they were known as locally, or sometimes 'two-year wonders'. They came full of ideas, some frankly exploitative, some with ideas about helping the locals, almost all siphoning off their profits in ways that did not in the long run benefit the island much. Perhaps he had just come in as emergency crew after the storm that had hit the West Indian chain of islands during the past days.

As though he'd read her thoughts, he favored her with a half-smile, giving nothing away. Jan found herself watching the way his eyes crinkled up at the corners. 'Maybe someone will start on it tomorrow, maybe the day after,' he said. 'Not today, for sure. It's a major job…weeks of work there to build a new road.'

'"Soon come," as the Jamaicans say,' she commented, with a token smile.

He shrugged eloquently in agreement. 'We try to be not quite as laid back,' he said.

'What am I going to do?' she said. 'I've come from Fort Roche. I've got two heavy bags. I don't want to drive all the way back again.' It was a rhetorical question. She certainly did not expect him to solve her problem, whoever he was.

There was no other road in to Manara, she knew that, only the dirt track that branched off the main road about a mile further on. So near and yet so far. Even if she drove back the way she had come and then took unpaved lanes to the other side of the island where it was only about four or five miles across, she could not get to Manara without hiking across country. Without the luggage that she had brought with her she might have tried it. There wasn't much point really. She may as well hike from this end where she would eventually link up with the track.

'Where are you heading?' he asked.

'There's a place called Manara—the plantation house.' She made a sweeping gesture in the general direction of her father's plantation. 'It's about a mile or so along this

road, then about two more miles inland along a dirt track
and—'

'I know it,' he interjected curtly, withdrawing his arms
from their support and stepping away from the van. 'I suggest you drive back to town and try again in a few days.
There might be some sort of temporary bypass road by
then. With things as they are, the track to the house may
not be clear. Even when the mud's cleared off the road
there's no guarantee that a vehicle could get through.'

'I can't drive back. My father's sick. I have to get in
there.' Jan made up her mind then, a little irritated by the
slightly dictatorial manner of this unknown male, a feeling
of desperation overlying her tiredness as she contemplated
the empty road up ahead.

At the same time her common sense told her he was
right. 'I fully understand what you've been telling me about
the danger, but I can't wait another two or three days.
Besides, I'm hot, tired and hungry. I'm not sure I'd survive
the journey back.'

Jan gave the man a slight smile, the best she could muster
under the circumstances, staring into his face which seemed
somewhat implacable to her at that moment. A frown
creased the skin between his strong, black eyebrows.

'Get out,' he commanded her, and jerked his head sideways decisively, indicating that she should do it in a hurry
and stop wasting his time. 'I'll see if I can arrange something with one of the workmen here to get this van back
to town. Then we'll find some way of getting you through
to the house. Are you Jack Newsome's daughter?'

'Yes,' Jan said, surprised relief making her voice breath-
less. 'Thank God you know him. Is he…is he all right?
He's been cut off.'

'He was all right when I saw him four days ago,' the
man replied, not adding the reason for his visit.

Jan got out of the van, her legs stiff. The air was pleasantly hot, tempered by a small breeze. In the pocket of her skirt she had a squashy cotton sun hat, which she pulled out and plonked firmly on her head. Together with the sunglasses it would shield her face from the hot early afternoon sun.

'We've been relatively unscathed by the storm, compared with two or three of the other islands,' the man said, his deep voice firm as he once again looked her over, noting her petite form. 'We had some heavy seas and torrential rain, but not much of the high winds that have caused a lot of damage on some of the other islands.'

As though on a cue, they both looked up at the brilliant sky, now an innocent blue, with only a few white, fluffy clouds evident in the distance.

'You saw my father?' Jan queried again, as she pulled her skirt free from her thighs, to which it seemed to be glued by sweat. 'I've been so worried…'

'Yes. I know Jack pretty well,' the man said. 'He's a bit of a workaholic, as you'll know. He was working as usual.'

'That's good to hear,' Jan said, squinting up at him, something of her sick anxiety easing. 'Now I can admit that it's good to be back on St Bonar, even in the present circumstances. I could always walk to Manara.' She turned, eyeing the dense foliage. 'I know the way from here.'

It would be an enjoyable walk, if long, through the quiet banana groves and the occasional cluster of coconut palms, where there might be a few skinny, tethered cows for company and many flitting birds in the trees and undergrowth. She longed to see the flowers at Manara.

'Forget that,' the man said, his voice harsher, looking at her with one hand on his hip, as though he could not quite figure her out. Jan felt dwarfed by him.

'I know this area very well. Practically grew up here. There are lots of paths,' she said.

'Sure,' he said, 'like the proverbial back of your hand, I

guess.' He smiled slightly. 'So do I know it. But I wouldn't recommend it after a storm, which does tend to alter the landscape. Unless you've got a death wish or something.'

He stood squarely in front of her, big and powerful. To her imagination, stimulated by the riot of color around her, he seemed rather like a larger-than-life character in an adventure movie, the type where the hero goes out to look for the Holy Grail or something like that.

She looked at him properly then, at his light, check shirt, open to the waist, and at his cotton pants which had once been white. These were streaked now with mud, the bottoms tucked into rubber boots. His face could have been called handsome if it were not composed in such stern lines, the sensual mouth serious again as though he had personally witnessed most of the sorrows of mankind on this earth.

'I'd like to live a little longer,' she said.

'Sure you would. This isn't the only landslide,' he added. 'We've explored some of this area. There are other parts that are not safe. If you come a cropper there may not be anyone around to help you out.'

Swashbuckling! That was the word that now came to Jan's mind. A wonderful word from her childhood, when she had spent some time on St Bonar, reminiscent of romantic stories of pirates and treasure buried in caves on lonely land-locked beaches. It all seemed another lifetime away.

'Mmm.' She nodded.

'The van can't be left here,' he said decisively, shifting his weight indolently from one hip to the other as though he were used to harangues in the middle of the road. 'For one thing, it could get broken into. For another, it will be in the way when the men want to bring a bulldozer along here tomorrow or the day after.'

'I've got to get there somehow,' Jan said.

'I'll have to go with you,' he said, 'so it's about time I introduced myself. I'm Gerard de Prescy. I'm temporarily part of the emergency committee that deals with storm damage...among other things.'

'I'm Janine Newsome,' she said formally as she took his proffered hand. Ruefully she acknowledged that she wanted to keep him at a psychological distance, as well as a physical one, if she could. Don't get involved, however temporarily, the familiar warning voice whispered to her. To her friends and family she was Jan.

His name jogged a vague memory. 'Were you here two years ago? I think I may have heard of you.'

'Yes,' he said, declining to elaborate.

For a moment her hand stayed in his, as though she did not have the strength to pull it away. His was firm, warm and rough. Here was a man who was clearly not used to directing operations from an office desk, she thought. The sensation of it was unexpected.

Jan withdrew her hand slowly from his grasp. 'Have you got time to come with me?' She frowned up at him. 'I don't want to impose on your time. There must be an awful lot to do.'

'I'll make time,' he said curtly. 'I wouldn't have offered otherwise.'

'Well...I appreciate it, very much,' Jan said, uncertain how to thank him. 'I...suppose you're an engineer or something?' she added, filling a small, awkward void between them. Maybe he was one of those developers who came to St Bonar frequently.

'No,' he said.

'Hello!' They heard themselves hailed, not having noticed the West Indian man who had approached from the direction of the clearance works.

With a laconic movement of an arm the newcomer caught the horse, which had wandered to the other side of the road, its reins trailing down. Leading the horse, he came up to them. 'Any problems, Mr de Prescy?' He was a thin, wiry man, clad in muddy work clothes, with the requisite rubber boots and a hard hat.

'A bit of a problem, Joseph,' her companion said, 'This lady has to get to Manara. We need someone to drive the van back to town. Do you think one of the men could do it? I'll have to go with her, take the horse.'

'Well, thank you. I didn't expect—' Jan began.

'I'll drive the van, Mr de Prescy,' Joseph offered quickly, hitching up his baggy, mud-stained pants in anticipation of getting behind the wheel.

Jan suppressed a smile. The men of St Bonar, who were generally excellent drivers, loved to speed along the narrow, tortuous, unpaved roads of the island. Numerous rusting hulks, abandoned throughout the landscape, attested to this. Not many people here could afford to own a car, so they seldom passed up an opportunity to drive one.

'I'm immensely grateful.' Jan smiled at the newcomer, knowing instinctively that the van would be safe with him. 'I hired it from the Tip Top garage on Bridge Street in Fort Roche All the papers are in the glove compartment.' She thought of the little garage, the size of a garden shed, where she had hired the van in town. 'They'll be surprised to see it back so soon. What about my luggage?' She addressed the question to neither man in particular.

Because Gerard de Prescy knew her father, Jan felt she could trust him. She felt herself drop some of the cynicism that she had been forced to acquire in her city life, yet it would be naïve to forget that she didn't know him, she reminded herself.

'We'll strap it to the horse,' de Prescy said, turning away abruptly.

When she had opened the van again the men busied themselves, tying her two bags, like saddlebags, to the sides of the resigned horse with rope they produced from a bag hanging over the saddle, while she slung the airline cabin bag over her shoulder.

The sun struck hot on her bare arms as she watched them, and she could feel the skin burning. It would be a good idea, she decided, to take this opportunity to smother any exposed areas of her body with sun-screen lotion, then take a drink from the water bottle she carried in her bag. With this in mind, she walked the few yards to the bend in the road and the shade of a thorn tree on the opposite side, where she had a view of the ocean.

Feeling a little bemused by the somewhat unaccustomed taking-over of her immediate affairs by two members of the opposite sex, she absently smoothed the lotion onto her bare arms. She could hear the two men talking, but could not make out what they were saying. Not that she was un-grateful for the help, far from it. It was just that she was, Jan told herself with some pride, used to standing very firmly on her own two feet. Turning away from them, she looked into the distance far out to the Caribbean Sea, where sunlight glistened on the very blue water like millions of diamonds.

'Spectacular, isn't it?' A voice sounded just behind her. Jan was startled. 'Er—yes,' she answered.

Gerard de Prescy had come up behind her silently as she stood on a small promontory under the tree. Beside her, he seemed very large, very masculine, giving her an unaccustomed sense of vulnerability and making her aware of her physical smallness. Hastily, Jan looked away from him to where the elevated land afforded a superb view of the ocean before them beyond a spread of banana trees. The blue water reflected the brilliance of the sky.

Over to their left, in the near distance, they could make out a wide, curving bay where the breakers crashed onto a deserted beach of white sand, where a small town was built down over the side of a hill, aptly named Eden Bay. White houses, mostly with red-painted corrugated tin roofs, were dotted here and there, looking like tiny dolls' houses, while the ones closer to the shore were of bright pastel colors. From this high vantage point they looked like bright little cardboard boxes with windows and doors painted on them.

'I love this view,' she burst out enthusiastically to this stranger, ignoring an underlying tension that seemed to hover between them. Or was that her imagination?

There seemed to be no one about down there, the only obvious movement being from the white-tipped waves that invaded the shore. It seemed untouched by the hurricane also, a sleepy, ageless place, basking in the heat.

'It is beautiful,' he agreed.

'If it weren't for the palm trees,' she went on, 'and the huge Catholic church, it could almost be Devon or Cornwall in Britain—with those huge rocks out there in the sea. I thought that when I first saw it when I was about four years old.' Jan wanted to share her joy. 'I spent a lot of summers here—some winters, too—when I was growing up.'

'Where was home?'

'England, mostly,' she said, 'though I'm in the States now because I've done some post-grad training there. We have some family there.' He was, she sensed, curious about her, but was trying not to show it too much.

The area before them was so different from the flatter land a little further north, where hotels for tourists had been built on many of the most beautiful beaches.

Just then the engine of the minibus burst into life under the apparently enthusiastic hands of Joseph. As Jan turned she took a few steps forward, impelled by a sudden odd sense of panic at the realization that she would be left alone with Gerard de Prescy.

The van shot forward in a cloud of smoke from the exhaust. It executed a neat U-turn and, as though shot from a cannon, roared at great speed down the short stretch of road, before rounding the bend that took it out of sight. There was a distant squeal of tires on tarmac, then they were left in relative silence.

'Don't worry, he's a good driver,' Gerard de Prescy said casually. 'Appearances can be deceiving.' There was a touch of humor in his voice.

'Yes...I'm sure he is.'

In the slightly uneasy void left by Joseph's departure with her lifeline to the town, Gerard de Prescy casually took a pair of sunglasses from the pocket of his shirt and put them on. 'I do quite a lot of my work in Eden Bay,' he said, appearing to sense her tension. 'I'm a doctor.'

'Oh... You are?' Jan's vision of him was forced into an abrupt change. To her he did not look like a doctor or, rather, not like the stereotyped version of a doctor. He was big, muscular, powerful...and at this moment rather dirty. 'You should have said so earlier.'

'You seemed to have me pegged as something else,' he said astutely. 'One of those "twelve-month wonders" perhaps?'

Jan flushed. 'Something like that,' she said, with an awkward laugh.

'Now you can relax,' he said. 'We're two of a kind, I understand. Your father told me you're a doctor. Have you got your MD already?'

'Yes. I've just finished a post-graduate course in general surgery. I also did some electives in pediatrics and obstetrics before that.'

'I'm impressed. You must be older than you look. To me, you look like a mere child.'

'Well, I'm not,' she asserted. That emphasis brought back a tension between them, which Jan told herself she was exaggerating. It was just that she was used to meeting men these days in a very definite, controlled setting, where each one had a defined role. To step outside that role had to be a very deliberate choice. Now she felt the boundaries shifting, that choice being taken somehow out of her hands, in the presence of this very masculine man.

'Shall we go?' he said. 'The horse doesn't belong to me, by the way. I have it on trust so we have to take good care of it.' As Jan watched, he untethered the horse.

'I'm surprised the poor thing didn't have a cardiac arrest, galloping after me in this heat,' she ventured.

'I note that you express no such concerns where I'm concerned, Miss Newsome,' he retorted, smiling at her. The humor made his face look softer momentarily, surprisingly attractive. 'You can be the pathfinder, and I'll take the horse for now.'

'Have you really got time for this?' she said. 'I feel guilty, taking up your time.'

'Let's call it accident prevention, shall we? That's a very big part of my job too. I'd like to see how Jack is as well.'

They began to walk, leading the horse. 'When is your father expecting you, Janine?' Gerard de Prescy queried, her name sounding lyrical the way he said it.

'I didn't give him a specific time,' Jan explained. 'He just knows I'm coming soon.'

Perhaps it was just as well that her father didn't know exactly when she was coming, had only known approximately when she would be leaving Boston. As it was, he would be worried.

Anxiety about the state of her father's general health came back to her, accompanied by worrisome thoughts about whether the storm had left him safe and Manara unscathed. She was concerned about the financial troubles that he had written of in his imprecise, rambling letters to her over the past few weeks, indicating that he might have to sell the plantation which had been in their family since 1875. He had also mentioned them during their telephone conversations, although he was always rather vague.

Soon they were off the road and into the welcome shade of large trees, searching for a path that Jan knew was there.

'Give me that bag,' Gerard said, as he came up easily beside her, leading the horse. 'We might as well put it with the others.'

For a few seconds his fingers brushed her arm as he lifted the bag over her head. 'You're going to need all your energy for walking once we're in the woods. We'll have to take frequent breaks and plenty of fluids. We don't want to go down with heat exhaustion.'

Jan felt herself tense at his touch, then found that she could think of nothing to say while he secured the bag to the saddle.

'Thank you,' she said at last.

'Call me Gerard,' he said. 'The locals call me Dr Gerard.'

'What if I don't want to go with you?' she said over her shoulder as they started walking again. 'After all, I don't know you.'

'You'll be quite safe with me,' he drawled. 'Joseph will have told the men by now who you are and where you're going—with me. Pretty soon half the island will know it. I've been here for almost three years—they all know me.'

She had to accept that. It was a little late to back out anyway.

He matched his pace to hers as they walked, the horse plodding along resignedly beside him. In spite of his fatigue, he walked easily, while Jan found herself panting a little already. The thought occurred to her that if the offer of a temporary job on St Bonar panned out she could well be working with this man in some capacity—a man who could be, she suspected, surprisingly opinionated. As it was, she found herself, without being sure why exactly, trying to harden her heart stubbornly against him. Perhaps John Clairmont had a lot to answer for...

For a time they walked in silence. The sun beat down on them and the smell of horse, mingling with the other pungent scents of the island, evoked in Jan an almost unbearable sense of nostalgia. To give up all this would not be easy.

Normally, it was easygoing in the banana plantations. Usually, all anyone had to do was simply walk between trees that were planted in rows in the soft, crumbly earth. Many of the flimsy trees had blown down in the storm, blocking these natural pathways. Jan waded through the long, fan-like leaves. It was not so easy for her companion, having to coax the reluctant horse to step over them. From time to time she heard him swear.

CHAPTER TWO

'HANG on!' The crude imperative brought Jan to a halt after they had been walking for some time. 'There's a machete in the saddlebag. I'll go ahead and hack a path for the horse. It's hard going, trying to drag her through this mess. You take the bridle.'

Jan nodded her assent. 'It gets flatter a little further on,' she said as she looked around carefully, assessing where they were with a fair degree of accuracy.

Gerard gave a noncommittal murmur. As they changed places, and he began to chop a pathway for them, she coaxed the horse forward. A renewed gratitude to this man, who was a stranger in an oddly intimate situation, edged its way into Jan's consciousness. Going it alone would have been near to impossible.

No doubt he did have other things he should be doing, more important things than going with her to Manara. Even so, she could not get it out of her mind that maybe he had other reasons for helping her. It was a strange intuition that she had been mulling over for the last half hour.

He would have to stay the night at Manara. Darkness descended at about half past six on St Bonar, and there was no way he could get out again before dark. The idea of having him there under the same roof overnight, in her father's house, was disturbing. She had wanted some quiet time alone with her father yet, if they found her father unwell, it would help to have another doctor on the scene.

'It's downhill a bit from now on,' she called to him, when they seemed to have been walking for hours, remembering from her past the lie of the land with uncanny accuracy, in spite of superficial changes. 'Then it levels out. Would you like some water? I've got some in my bag.'

'Wait till we get down to the level. We'll take a break there.' An odd, reluctant camaraderie was springing up between them.

When they began to slither down an incline to more even ground he came to help her with the horse as it braced itself for the descent. For the last few yards they let it go, to plunge forward to a wider path lower down, which was mercifully clear of fallen trees as far as they could see.

'Give me your hand,' Gerard said, as they inched their way forward down the steepest part of the incline, which was covered with brush, small trees and fallen leaves. He was slightly ahead of her and he turned to help her. The roughness of his hand, clammy with moisture, made her feel reassured and at the same time vulnerable as they carefully negotiated the same path that the horse had taken.

'Oh…' Jan let out a cry as her foot slid from under her on a patch of moist soil and she fell with a thud flat on her back, winded, pulling at his hand which was still gripping hers. With a muffled exclamation, Gerard fell heavily with her, his body half covering hers.

They lay panting, his weight pinning her to the ground, which was moist and surprisingly cool on her back. With his arms on either side of her body, as he had fallen, his face was almost touching her own. Jan felt her whole body stiffen away from him as his masculine scent filled her nostrils.

Gasping for breath, she willed her body to relax against the cool earth. Her hands were at her sides, the fingers digging ineffectually into the loose soil.

'Are you all right?' He ground out the words with effort.

'I…think so…Yes,' Jan panted, aware only of his weight—his proximity—on her. There was no pain anywhere in her body. They lay where they were, unable to move, listening to the horse snorting below them on the path.

'The horse...' Jan whispered.

'She won't go anywhere,' he said, resting his forehead on the ground beside her shoulder.

'Are you all right?' Jan ventured after a moment.

'Yeah,' he said. 'Just winded.'

Above her, through the canopy of trees, Jan could see patches of blue sky. Only a little of the intense heat penetrated the cool shade where they lay. Gradually, as her breathing quietened she became aware of the rapid pounding of her heart, then of his heartbeat where the left side of his chest pressed against her soft breasts.

Although she could have moved then, a languor held her immobile. The quiet of the woods and the bird calls formed a bower of sight and sound which was enchanting.

Move! she commanded herself silently.

Before she could obey her own admonition Gerard lifted his head and looked at her, his face very close to hers so that she could look into his dark, unfathomable eyes. Slowly those eyes went over her face, feature by feature.

'You're very beautiful, Janine Newsome,' he said, almost absently. 'Grubby, but beautiful all the same.'

Those words disarmed her with their unexpectedness. That, and a muted light of admiration in his eyes—something she had not seen on the face of a man in recent months—made her close her eyes in acquiescence when his lips came down on hers.

His mouth was warm and firm and explored hers without demand, uninhibitedly taking pleasure from her. Sensing his need and his enjoyment of her, she felt herself respond against her will, felt herself give in to the sharp flare of sexual attraction that seemed to spark between them.

Her arms came around him, her fingers making contact with the moist heat of his body through the thin material of his shirt. Unable to help herself, she returned his kiss, giving herself up to it mindlessly.

For a long time they did not break contact. Actual time lost all significance. Gerard moved a hand to touch her hair, to stroke it away from her forehead, and she moaned involuntarily with a need that had been suppressed for too long.

He eased himself slightly away from her and his free hand gently traced the outline of her breast, his thumb brushing her bare skin where the blouse gaped open at the top before he moved that hand to prop himself up. He did it so lightly that it could almost have been accidental. Her senses flared into acute awareness.

I must get up... The words formed themselves in her stupefied brain. The pleasure of his touch kept her still, her hands pulling him against her.

It was the whinnying of the horse that brought them back to a sharp realization that time was passing. Darkness fell early on St Bonar. When Gerard pulled away from Jan she opened her eyes to see undisguised desire on his face before he sat up abruptly, smoothing his tangled hair away from his face.

Lying there and looking at his broad back, Jan felt stunned. She had wanted him to make love to her...still wanted him. In a way it was shocking. He was a stranger, he could be married. Yet she could not censure herself. A sharp sense of loss at the broken physical contact dominated everything else.

When he got up abruptly and held out a hand to her his face was expressionless. 'Come on,' he said, 'we'd better get going. I hadn't planned for that sort of break.'

The touch of humor in his voice turned a potentially awkward situation into something that seemed perfectly natural...at least for now. No doubt some sort of embarrassment would surface later, Jan admitted to herself as she followed him down the incline. They had both silently admitted a need…that the other could satisfy.

At the bottom of the hill, where the earth was relatively dry, Gerard stripped off his shirt, stuffing it into a saddle-bag. Sweat and dirt had left runnels down his tanned back and chest, his firm, muscled flesh shiny with heat. Silently he handed her a water bottle, together with a plastic cup.

'This is very civilized.' She tried to make it sound light, indicating the cup. She found that she was having trouble meeting his eyes, shaken by the unexpected kiss.

'Take as much as you want,' he said. 'I'll swig from the bottle.'

'Thanks. I have some too.' The cool water was good.

'Your father telephoned you to come here. Right?' he queried as he busied himself with the horse, tightening the ropes on her luggage.

'Yes. I…I'm closer, you see, in Boston. My mother's in England. That's their permanent home. They spend three to six months of the year here.' Jan chattered, trying to divert the focus away from the physical contact they had shared. 'Usually she's with him, but her own mother's not well and she's nursing her so I don't want to worry my mother until I know there's something to really worry about.'

'Mmm. I know he has a manager and staff, who look after the place when he's not here. They run the business.'

'Yes. My father also seems to think that because I'm a doctor I can wave a magic wand or something and make everything all right.'

'And your own job?' he said.

'I've got leave of absence. They won't hold it open for me indefinitely, of course. I should think that the three months I'm taking would be the limit.'

'You're specialized in surgery?'

'Yes.'

'Mmm.'

'He—my father—has a stomach ulcer,' Jan explained, feeling on safer ground now that they were discussing professional matters. 'The problem is—he neglects his own health. He lets things go until there's a crisis.'

'Sounds familiar,' he murmured.

'All his energies go into running and conserving the plantation, which he inherited from his father,' she went on, 'so this will be my opportunity to see just what treatment he's getting—make sure that he's had a test for stomach bacteria, the *Helicobacter pylori*, then he can have the appropriate treatment.'

'We haven't got the antibody serology test available here yet. We've no pathologist or microbiologist here either. We have to send pathology specimens out to one of the bigger islands,' he said.

'I brought a breath test kit with me,' she said. 'As I expect you know, the bacteria produce a chemical that can be detected in the breath.' Her voice trailed off as she fiddled with the water bottle, not wanting to play the bossy young thing from the big city preaching to an ignoramus from the back of beyond. She felt sure he was as up-to-date as she was on the discoveries of the causes and treatment of bacteria-induced stomach ulcers.

'Hmm,' he said, noting her discomfiture, a hint of amusement in his voice, 'I hope you brought a few recent medical journals with you. I could use a few. We keep in touch via the Internet here, but it's largely a matter of having enough time.'

Knowing that she had been talking quickly to divert herself from her sharp awareness of him and from the fact that they were alone, Jan began to brush leaves and bits of soil from her clothing. When she glanced at him there was no hint in his features that he was teasing her about the journals or that he felt any embarrassment. She knew that she had had a tendency to be on the defensive ever since her romantic fiasco with John Clairmont.

'How come Don McLean hasn't been treating your father?' Gerard de Prescy asked, clearly puzzled.

'My father didn't admit to him that he had any symptoms,' she said.

'I see. Have you had all you want of the water?' he said, changing the subject. When she handed him the water bottle he drank what was left of it, pouring it down his throat with scarcely a swallow.

Although he couldn't be more than about thirty-five, Jan decided, he had deep lines in his forehead and at the corners of his eyes, as though he had spent much time squinting against the sun. His hair, moistened by sweat and liberally sprinkled with small pieces of debris from fallen trees, was as tangled as her own, falling in little curling tendrils over his forehead in a way that made him look almost boyish.

'This is my habitual appearance these days,' he said a little brusquely, seeing her quick, assessing regard, as a renewed flare of attraction passed between them.

Instinctively Jan sensed a slight wariness in him and looked away. A man with a past, perhaps, she speculated. Perhaps a past much like her own, with the female equivalent of John? She had become adept at reading the signs, however well hidden.

'My father should have a gastroscopy,' she said, feeling safer with medical matters, 'and a stomach biopsy to rule out cancer. I assume that can be done here? I just have to persuade him.'

'Yeah, that can be done here, although we would have to send the biopsy specimen offshore. There's only one pathologist for several islands,' he said.

'Everything seems to have deteriorated here,' she commented as they resumed walking. 'Everything man-made, that is.' They both felt the need to talk, to mute the awareness of the other's proximity.

'Yeah...the economic downturn has taken its toll here, like everywhere else,' he said. 'Bananas and coconuts are not exactly staples in the world's diet. Tourism's down badly.'

Jan found herself looking sideways at his angular, uncompromising profile. What, she wondered, had brought him to this small island in the Caribbean? Obviously he partially belonged here...he had the accent that could never be faked.

There were so many questions she wanted to ask him— why he was on the island, where he had come from. Her newly acquired reticence, where men were concerned, kept her silent.

It took them another half-hour of walking before they came in sight of Manara. The going was easier, in a slight valley most of the way, and appeared to have been sheltered from the storm, the pathway being wide and largely unencumbered by debris.

They scarcely spoke, concentrating on putting one foot in front of the other. Jan led the way again, keeping ahead of Gerard and the horse. From time to time, to her surprise, he sang snatches of songs—old French love songs, as far as she could make out, which would be in keeping with the colonial history of the island, both French and British.

As she listened to the sound, to the words that she barely understood, and felt her body tingle with the memory of the long, lingering kiss they had just shared, Jan knew intuitively that she had missed out on something important in her life, something that she had not had time for—not even with John. Maybe especially not with John. The insight came to her with a sharp poignancy.

There had been plenty of men in her life, some serious. No, it was not male contact that she had missed out on.

Their careers had always come first with those men, that was it. It seemed now that they had scarcely seen her as a woman, except as someone who would, perhaps, fulfill their sexual needs.

Gerard de Prescy, for those brief minutes, had made her feel like a woman, and had tacitly acknowledged her womanly needs, had exposed his own needs. There was something about this island that always brought you back to a basic, intuitive reality, yet she could not succumb to it—or to him. She was only here temporarily.

This man was an enigma, seemingly a mixture of many nations. The songs took her mind off her renewed thirst, aching legs and the prickly heat.

Then there it was, the old plantation house, standing faded and magnificent in front of them in a clearing. It looked at once out of place in the surrounding wild vegetation and at the same time so much a part of it. Lit by the shafting late afternoon sun, it looked solid and enduring.

'There's the house!' she exclaimed, unnecessarily, jubilation overcoming her tiredness. 'It's magnificent...still!'

As always, Jan felt her spirits surge and a nostalgic tightening of her throat at the sight of it, as though she might cry. The relief of their safe arrival was mixed with an equal relief in knowing that she would soon be released from the disturbing closeness of Gerard de Prescy.

'Any idea why it's called Manara?' He had come up beside her on the path.

They stopped to rest and stared at the house that was a few hundred yards ahead of them, panting from their exertions. The air was pleasantly warm under the trees, a breeze caressing Jan's bare limbs like a touch of velvet.

'There's a story that it was the name of a woman, the daughter of a former slave, who was loved by the plantation owner,' Jan said slowly, recalling the history. 'She was a servant here. Before that it was called La Belle Maison.

Apparently, Manara had several children by him, then died of cholera in an epidemic in about 1854 and was buried here. He named the house after her and asked to be buried with her when he died.'

'And was he?' Like her, he was breathing heavily from the exertion.

'There is a grave...on a hill with a view to the sea. It only has his name on it—Henri Daviot. It's on the property.'

'Yes...Daviot...' He repeated the name absently. 'I knew they owned this place at one point. Very interesting. I guess it goes without saying that he didn't marry her?' There was a subtle cynicism in his voice.

'Mmm...He didn't marry her, as far as I know,' she confirmed. 'I think he had a wife he'd left behind in France.'

'I guess she was what the locals would call an "outside wife",' Gerard de Prescy commented. 'It was a common arrangement...still goes on today. Some men have several outside wives in different locations.'

'So I understand,' Jan murmured, as she found herself querying again whether this very masculine man at her side was married and whether he had any outside wives. For a few moments the unbidden speculation came to her mind of what it might be like to be married to him...

'A very amicable and civilized arrangement,' he murmured, interrupting her thoughts, 'in a place that is considered by outsiders as not particularly civilized. Provided it's mutual, of course. In the 1850s it probably wasn't.'

Jan made no comment on that, aware of an absurd fear that he could read her thoughts. She had felt reluctant, too, to repeat the sad story to him, a story which had been all too common almost a century and a half ago when disease had come swiftly and fatally, a time made 'romantic' only by the passage of years. Many of the plantation owners in the past had taken 'out women', as they had been called then, particularly those whose women had not come to the islands with them from Europe.

'You sound very knowledgeable on the subject,' Jan commented.

He turned to look at her, his eyes going over her from her head down to her feet and slowly back again. He had removed his sunglasses in the shade of the trees. It was a dark, assessing look that caused Jan to catch her breath and feel momentarily as though she were suffocating, as though she were being pulled into the compelling orbit of his will.

'Sure,' he agreed, 'I've studied the history of this island. And there's something about this climate that makes it seem right. Wouldn't you agree? As a partial child of the islands?' He smiled, his black eyebrows raised above penetrating eyes that seemed as deep as the brown depths of a forest stream. There was an invitation in those depths, subtle yet unmistakable.

Jan swallowed, very aware of him. Was he teasing her? 'Is that an invitation?' she said, forcing a lightness to her voice, while all her civilized instincts told her not to get involved with him.

'It can be...if you want it to be,' he challenged softly.

Jan looked away towards the house, conscious of her heart beating a steady, deep rhythm.

'Cholera was pretty common here then,' he said, deliberately easing the tension. 'People died like flies in the epidemics...in their thousands.'

'Yes...'

'Do you know Father Jessop, the Catholic priest at the cathedral in Forte Roche? He's the island historian and archivist, as well as being a priest.'

'Yes...I do know him,' Jan said, thinking of the local man who did so much that was good on the island, a scholar and practical man combined.

'He's doing some family research for me. I have connections to these islands, to England and to France, as well as to the States. As you know, island people move around a lot... Many come back.' There was an odd note to his voice that made Jan look at him sharply.

'Henri Daviot.' He repeated the name slowly, 'Obviously not a family ancestor of yours, with a name like that?'

'No, a Frenchman. The plantation was a gift from a French king, I believe, to a Daviot ancestor...long before my great-great-grandfather bought the plantation. Daniel Newsome... He was a merchant seaman, the source of our wonderful inheritance...or all our troubles, whichever way you want to look at it.'

'An Englishman?'

'Mmm...'

'And did she love this Henri in return...the slave woman?' he queried softly.

Jan shrugged, pretending casualness, whereas, in fact, the story had always touched her deeply, as it did now. Also, she was surprised at his interest. 'One hopes so,' she said. 'Some indications are there that he did. His epitaph would indicate that.'

He did not ask her what it was so she did not go on.

Since first hearing something of the story as a child, she had hoped that the liaison had been a passionate mutual love, then after the first flush of her own youthful naïvety had passed and she had acquired a greater knowledge of island history she had had to concede that there could have been an element of coercion. However, from the epitaph, which Jan knew by heart, there seemed little doubt that Henri had loved the woman.

'And the children... Did they die of cholera?' Gerard de Prescy persisted, his shrewd glance alternating between the beautiful old house in the near distance and her dishevelled person next to him. He raked dirty fingers through his own hair, picking out bits of twigs and leaves.

'No one seems to know. Maybe some of them died…maybe some of them escaped to France,' she answered.

'Father Jessop has told me that perhaps I am related in some way to the Daviot family,' he said. 'There's a lot more research to be done, though.'

'Really!' she said, turning to him in surprise. 'That's… fascinating. When will you know?'

He shrugged. 'He's waiting for his contacts in France to report back. Most of the family remained in France, apparently. Only Henri was here for any length of time.'

They walked towards the house, taking it slowly now.

'I suspect that your father finds Manara too much of an effort now,' Gerard said, squinting across the distance they had yet to go and appraising the old house. 'He's reluctant to admit it directly.'

'You're right. You seem to know my father rather well.'

'We've met many times,' he said. He was fully aware, then, Jan sensed, of her efforts to sum him up. He seemed to be standing back, watching her struggle with it—a struggle that afforded him some amusement. 'Things move on, you know, when you're not here. I'd like to think he regards me as a friend.' There was a hint of something that she could not fathom.

'But you didn't know he was unwell?'

'He didn't tell me,' he replied curtly, 'From pride, I suspect. There's a limit to how far one can interfere in someone else's life, Janine.'

Closer to the house, as they approached along an overgrown footpath, Jan could see how much the place had deteriorated. The basic structure—the walls two feet thick to withstand hurricanes, built very solidly of coral stone covered with stucco—had an enduring quality, yet the pale yellow paint on the stucco of the large, square, two-story house was peeling badly. Much of the woodwork was bleached bare by seasons of harsh sunlight.

The gracefully proportioned house had many tall, elegant windows which suggested high ceilings inside. Some of the shutters on these windows, and the wooden slatted jalousies that lifted upwards on the smaller windows, once a bright green, were faded now. Some of them hung on loose hinges. There was an air of benign neglect, a sadness. Vegetation from the surrounding woodland was encroaching on the lawns and gardens, running rampant with vibrant life.

Only the flowers—the cultivated bougainvillea growing up over the verandahs to the roof and cascading down in fronds of brilliant pinks and mauves, the hibiscus near the entrance steps, the creamy pink oleander growing along the front—saved the shabbiness from being pathetic.

As they approached the house a Range Rover came along the main track, suddenly appearing from among tall trees, and pulled up at the front of the house.

'Looks like Jack's all right,' Gerard de Prescy commented.

'Thank God!' The words came out on a sob. 'Dad! Dad!' Jan began to run, waving her arms as she stumbled through the vegetation that brushed her ankles.

The man who got out saw them immediately and was obviously surprised. Then he waved and called, 'Jan!'

'Hullo, Dad,' Jan called and smiled at her father's appearance, feeling immense relief that he was alive and apparently well... Well enough to drive, anyway. Tears formed in her eyes and spilled over onto her cheeks.

'Well, well! The prodigal returns,' he called out, holding his arms open with a welcoming grin as she ran towards him. The last time they had met had been in Boston, when he had called in on his way to St Bonar from England a few months before.

'Thank God.' She repeated the words, wiping at the tears with grimy hands before falling into his arms. They hugged tightly.

In spite of Jack Newsome's somewhat unusual way of life, part spent in England, part in St Bonar, he always managed to look like an insurance salesman. He usually wore a shirt, tie and neat trousers, whatever the circumstances. Now was no exception, albeit the tie was loose, the shirtsleeves rolled up and the trouser bottoms stuffed into rubber boots.

'Oh, Dad! How are you?' There was a wealth of meaning in those simple words. As they hugged she could feel how thin he had become.

'I'm fine,' Jack Newsome held his daughter at arm's length to get a good look at her, and smiled. With a sense of shock, which Jan hoped would not show on her face, she noted the hollows beneath his cheek-bones, the yellowish tinge to his skin and the tiredness in his pale blue eyes which were so like her own. 'I'm absolutely delighted and relieved to see you, Jan…you and Gerard…the two people I most wanted to see. Did you have much trouble getting here?'

Jan smiled at him, hastily blinking away the moisture in her eyes. 'Apart from the landslide here creating problems, everything else was more or less fine,' she said, glossing over her sporadic difficulties and delays.

Surreptitiously she again swept her eyes over her father's sparse frame when he let her go, noting how grey his still plentiful hair had become. She felt a stab of fear for him. Perhaps she had arrived just in time.

A shy man, normally not overtly demonstrative, Jack Newsome was clearly extremely pleased to see his daughter and have her company.

They both turned to look at the man who led the tired

horse, which was now snorting and pricking up its ears at
the expectation of having a well-earned rest and drink.

'Hello, Gerard.' Jan's father smiled a welcome, stepping
forward to greet the other man. They shook hands. 'Welcome to Manara once again. Great to see you! I won't ask
how you two came to be together until you've had a long,
cool drink. You both look as though you've had a rough
time.'

'We met on the road, literally. Your daughter was all set
to tramp through the woods on her own,' Gerard de Prescy
said evenly, his weathered face lighting up as he smiled at
her father.

'Ah...she would!' Jack Newsome grinned, putting his
arm around Jan's shoulders. 'Always stubborn, eh, Jan? Not
a good time to arrive, I'm afraid, with the awful weather
we've been having.' From his tone, she might have been
arriving for a holiday.

Jan did not comment that she intended to work on St
Bonar, after a few days of much needed rest. That would
come later. They needed money badly at Manara. The con-
stant need frequently cast a pall over this paradise.

Neither of them acknowledged that he had summoned
her there, had asked for help. She would speak to her father
privately about that.

'Good to see you, Jack,' Gerard de Prescy cut in. It
seemed to Jan that there was a definite professional interest
in the long, assessing look that he gave her father. 'How
have you been?'

'Well...I've been better,' Jack Newsome said. 'Maybe I
can get your professional advice later on.'

'Sure.'

'Come into the house,' her father invited them. 'I've got
a lot to tell you, Jan. I've been cut off here. Still am. I'm
without staff at the moment too. They've either gone to
take care of their families in this crisis or they're involved

in emergency clearance work. It's difficult for them to get back.'

'Is everything all right, Dad?' Jan said anxiously.

'Basically, yes,' her father said. 'I've got plenty of food on hand, all basic supplies, so I really don't have to go anywhere.'

'I'll just see to the horse first.' Gerard de Prescy untied the ropes holding Jan's bags on the horse and lifted them to the ground, before tethering the animal in the shade beside a water trough. They all stood and watched while it took a long drink, then Gerard doused his crumpled shirt with water and rubbed the horse down.

The two new arrivals, lugging the bags, followed Jack Newsome up the wide, crumbling stone steps to the solid mahogany front door of the house. On the top step he turned to them, encompassing them both in his glance, and announced calmly, 'I'm very glad you two have met... saves me a lot of explanation. Gerard, I guess you've told Jan that you've offered to buy Manara?'

He pushed the door open, preceding them into the interior from which emanated the slight scent of mustiness that commonly came after a heavy rain, mixed with the perfume of sandalwood.

'What? What do you mean, Dad?' Jan said. 'I didn't think you were serious about selling it.'

She dumped her bag inside the threshold of the house, where cool air was trapped in the wide hallway under high ceilings. As she put it down she had the sharp sense that she was shedding some burdens, only to take on others of a different nature. She looked around quickly at the familiar old mahogany furniture, which had once been very grand, and the threadbare oriental carpet.

'What do you mean?' she repeated.

As she looked at both men it was obvious that Gerard de Prescy was avoiding her scrutiny. Muscles rippled in his bare torso as he carried her two heavier bags with ease to the center of the capacious hall, before lowering them. Beside her father's thin frame he was a commanding presence, somehow bringing the dusty stillness of the large, old, neglected house to a renewed life, and she found herself resenting that.

'It's simply something that we've discussed, Jan,' her father said mildly. 'Come into the sitting room. I'm going to get you some lemon tea.'

Jack Newsome deliberately left them alone and Jan was glad, not wanting to get into an argument with Gerard in front of him.

Jan looked at Gerard de Prescy anew, anger burning in her. 'How come you didn't breathe a word about that to me, Dr de Prescy?' she said, her cheeks flushed with the recollection of how she had responded to his kiss. 'We spent all that time together and you didn't say anything?'

'I thought we had enough on our plate to contend with,' Gerard said, looking at her, 'without getting into a discussion about your father's affairs.'

'They are my affairs too,' Jan said, her voice shaking from exhaustion and anger. 'Perhaps my father didn't tell you that I'm part owner of Manara. It was left that way in my grandfather's will.'

The expression of surprise on his face told her that her father had not spoken of it. 'Is that right?' he said.

'Yes,' she said emphatically. 'He was probably hoping for some sort of continuity.' Jan thought of the grandfather she did not remember and whom she had only seen in photographs, who had died two years after she was born. 'Anyway, Dr de Prescy, any sale requires my signature.'

A sense of outrage had taken possession of her that he would assume that she, being a woman, perhaps, would not have any say in the legal affairs of the house. Was that why he had not mentioned it?

He had kissed her, touched her... The memory of his hand on her breast seemed to burn in her brain.

'I certainly didn't know that,' he said quietly. 'And will there be continuity? You're married? You have children?'

The penetrating look he gave her, when he must have guessed that she was not married because he had seen her ringless fingers, was, no doubt, calculated to remove some of the validity of her argument, Jan supposed. That shrewdness fueled her sense of outrage.

'No, I'm not married,' she said. 'At the moment, I represent the continuity.'

'You don't live here.'

'I could. It's also a business,' she retorted. 'Besides, I love this house.'

'The house isn't exactly for sale, Jan,' her father interrupted placatingly, having come back.

'Sorry, Dad, I didn't mean—'

'I know how much you love the place. I just said that Gerard had offered. It's something I've been thinking about in these last few months. This storm may just about finish us off, with our profit margin the way it is,' Jack Newsome went on quietly, reasonably. 'I've talked it over with Gerard and he offered to buy it. It's not irrevocable. Anyway, come and have a drink and something to eat... We can talk about this later.'

'Just a minute.' She turned to the other man, 'What would you want it for?'

This time he did not avoid looking at her. 'Partly because of the possible family connection with the Daviots that I spoke about earlier, and partly because I'm thinking of building a private clinic to attract patients from outside the island,' he said. 'People who would bring money here to St Bonar to help our economy.'

'What!'

'This property is one of three possible places I'm looking

at. I would live in the house and renovate it to provide accommodation for the guests as well, post-op and pre-op—who would also be the patients, of course,' he went on calmly. 'The house would essentially remain the same. We would need to have another building, with operating theatres, recovery areas, immediate post-op accommodation, laboratories, and so on.'

Jan looked from one man to the other. 'I'm not sure I like that idea,' she said, incredulous. 'Not with our house. What about the land?'

'Most of that would, we hope, remain in cultivation.' Her father was the one to answer. 'Some of the other islands are doing this, Jan. They're attracting plastic surgeons and their patients, mainly for cosmetic surgery, so I believe. It appeals to people who want to keep their face-lifts a secret. You have a holiday, you come back looking well rested and mysteriously younger.' Jack Newsome smiled, apparently trying to make the best of his altered circumstances—finding whatever humour he could in them.

Jan, stupefied, felt an incredible sadness that things had come to this, together with an anger at the younger man who seemed to her at that moment to be an opportunist, trading on her father's misfortunes. She frowned, looking from one to the other.

'They would also come,' her father went on, 'for something routine like a simple hernia operation, so Gerard assures me.'

He would! Jan thought cynically, looking at the doctor. 'And why would they want to come here?' She frowned at him again. 'To this island? It's not exactly one of the more sophisticated of the islands. They could go to the Caymans, or to Bermuda. And where would the surgeons come from?'

'That's what we have to work out,' he said. 'It can be done. We already have a list of those who might be seriously interested. Your father has a copy. I'm not saying it would work out at Manara—it's very tentative at the moment.'

'I've got some lemon tea in the kitchen,' her father said mildly. 'Come on through.'

As they turned to follow him, tears of tiredness and sadness formed in Jan's eyes. Relieved that her father was still walking around, she now felt a certain sense of betrayal. Confusion engendered by the powerful attraction she felt for this stranger left her momentarily at a loss.

Gerard de Prescy, seeing the moisture in her eyes, stopped in front of her. 'Don't do that,' he said gently. 'You're tired and overwrought. Everything's going to be all right.' With that, he left her, striding out of the hall as though he were already master of Manara.

Numbly Jan stood on the spot and looked around her, composing her features. How she had loved this place once! She knew now that she still did.

Sometimes recently she hadn't been sure. She had begun to realize of late that time did things to you, made you change. Sometimes it occurred against your will, sometimes without you understanding it until something happened to bring you face to face with your old self and the realization that something had changed in you also as well as in outside circumstances.

Feelings which had been vague in her were nudged suddenly into being, perhaps by her thoughts of John Clairmont, and came unbidden into slightly sharper focus as she looked around the familiar old hallway in those few seconds. Would she ever marry and have children, as her grandfather had wished, for the continuity of this place? As she wished herself?

This had been the place of arrival, this vast hallway, the gathering place for family holidays. It was a time that had gone for ever.

CHAPTER THREE

JAN was awake when the first fingers of dawn light showed through the louvered shutters of her bedroom to show up the outlines of the faded, much loved furniture and fabrics which had remained unchanged since her childhood. Much of it had been lovingly sewn or chosen by her mother, or inherited from the past.

It had taken her a while to fall asleep the night before, even though she had been exhausted. She and Gerard had eaten a light supper and had gone to bed early. The persistent 'peep, peep, peep' of the tree frogs, who started up their nightly chorus not long after darkness fell and were particularly active after a period of rain, had seemed louder than she remembered them.

Awake now, she thought about Dr John Clairmont. Here in this old familiar place she could view him differently from the way she had seen him in that high-tech hospital in Boston, a place that had been very much his territory, where she had been the outsider to a large extent—the foreigner, who had been very fortunate to get a post-graduate training position in surgery there.

To her he had seemed suave, handsome, sophisticated and a little spoiled, something she had overlooked then...had been willing to overlook, she realized now, because she had been attracted and fascinated by everything else that he had represented. Altogether, they had worked with each other for two years before the crisis. For nine months of those two years they had been lovers.

After they had split up she had had more post-MD surgery training to do. If John had not moved to another hospital she might not have completed it, the tension between them at work having been unbearable.

John had been arrogant, although not at first with her. He was the son of Roderick Clairmont, who was the head of the plastic and reconstructive surgery department at the hospital, a man widely respected and admired for his work and teaching abilities. Perhaps John, in general surgery himself, had coasted along a little on his father's reputation. Anyway, she had been captivated by him, as had several other women who, like her, had been doing training residencies in the hospital.

Jan stirred restlessly under the single sheet that covered her bed, thinking of that other doctor who now slept in her house here in St Bonar...a man with rough, work-worn hands, and a weathered face, as far from studied charm as a person could get. She remembered the exhaustion on his face and how they had come together in an explosive kiss... Could she trust him now she knew that he was interested in the house?

As she thought of Gerard de Prescy's touch on her heated skin, she knew, if she were honest, that she had wanted him to touch her. Maybe, at long last, it was time to get Dr Clairmont out of her system.

She and John had first met in the operating rooms, in the staff lounge, in the corridors and at meetings, then they had worked together. They had started dating, even though neither of them had had much free time. Then she had fallen in love for the first time in her life. There had been little thought at first of a shared future. For both of them, concentrating on their careers as they were, there had been a strong sense that they were living very much for the moment.

As time went by Jan found that gradually she had begun to think tentatively of a possible future together. The shock had come when she had realized that with him it had not been the case, that nothing had been further from his mind. Then there had been the consultation that had ruined things between them...

What she had not been prepared for had been his vindictiveness, his complete about-face where she was concerned, when he felt his career threatened. She had not been prepared for his hatred, to find out that he was a man she had not known in any way...having loved him. The shock to her faith in her own judgement had been devastating.

It had happened just over a year ago, that awful time. Jan allowed her clamoring thoughts to go back to the past when the budding relationship she had had with John Clairmont had come to an end, brought about by what had really been professional pique on his part, disguised as personal rejection...

She was a junior resident-in-training in post-grad general surgery in the city hospital and John was the senior resident. A call came out one evening for them to get to the emergency department fast to see a patient with serious internal bleeding. Jan was the first to get there and find the patient, a woman of thirty-two, almost exsanguinated from loss of blood, unable to give a history. The digital blood pressure and pulse rate monitor to which the patient was hooked up showed that the pressure was dangerously low, the pulse rapid.

'Has anyone done a vag. examination?' she asked the nurse.

'Yes. Nothing there.'

As Jan and the nurse frantically started intravenous fluids and a blood transfusion of uncrossmatched blood she questioned the boyfriend of the woman. The man, almost paralytic with fear, did not give good answers.

'Could she be pregnant, do you think?' Jan questioned, not looking up from the tasks on hand, while the nurse with her ripped open packs of I.V. fluid and passed her equipment.

'Well...she could be...I suppose,' he said hesitantly. 'Gee, I don't know... She didn't say anything like that to me. Oh, my God, my God. What do you think's wrong with her? Is she dying? For Christ's sake do something!'

'We are doing something, sir,' Jan said, moving as quickly as all her expertise would allow. The woman's veins were all but collapsed because of loss of blood pressure due to the haemorrhage.

By some miracle, Jan managed to get two intravenous cannulas in place for connecting to the tubing that would allow precious fluid to run into the woman's veins, hopefully raising her blood pressure before it became even more dangerously low which could result in brain and kidney damage.

'We'll need more blood,' she murmured to the nurse.

'I've got two more units on hand,' the nurse replied tersely, 'and I've ordered more. The I.V. technician from the lab has already taken blood for a crossmatch. They'll have that ready by the time they need it in the operating room.'

'Great!' Jan said. 'How did she get here?'

'By ambulance. Collapsed in a shopping mall. Had some abdominal pain. She's sure bleeding like heck from somewhere.'

The face of their patient was a ghastly blanched yellow colour, the lips tinged with gray.

'We should probably do a mini-laparotomy, maybe a laparoscopy also,' Jan said, speaking quickly as her thoughts ranged over all the possibilities, 'to see if she's bleeding into the abdominal cavity.'

'Sure,' the nurse said. 'I've got all the stuff on hand for that. I'll open it up as soon as we've done this.'

With a mini-laparotomy they would make a tiny incision

into the abdominal cavity, run in a litre of sterile I.V. fluid via a plastic tube, then siphon it back immediately. Any blood in the fluid would then be evident, and the whole procedure would only take a few minutes.

When the fluids were flowing freely into the patient's veins Jan straightened, looking the distraught boyfriend straight in the eyes. 'Stay calm,' she instructed sternly. 'This is very important. I ask you this question again. Could she possibly be pregnant?'

'Yes...yes...I guess she could,' he almost shouted. 'What the hell's going on?'

'She's bleeding very badly from somewhere inside,' Jan explained quickly and patiently as she palpated the patient's abdomen and the nurse readied the simple mini-laparotomy equipment. 'Obviously something has ruptured, including a major blood vessel. We'll have to take her to the operating room to find out...right now. The nurses have alerted the operating rooms that we're on our way. Everything is in motion, sir—'

That was as far as she got with the case. Dr John Clairmont came rushing in, his white lab coat billowing out behind him so that he looked like an avenging angel, to-gether with the senior resident on the chest surgery team. They were followed closely by the X-ray technician on call, pushing the portable X-ray machine that was always kept in the emergency department. John all but elbowed Jan aside, with barely a glance or an acknowledgement of what she had done so far.

'Make way,' he commanded, with that look of taut ex-citement he always had on his face when confronted with something challenging. 'We've got to get X-rays. Stat! Out of the way!'

'We have the mini-laparotomy equipment ready, Dr Clairmont,' the nurse said calmly, 'and the operating room's been informed. They're ready for us.'

'So they ought to be,' he snapped back. 'That's their job. I'm not going to bother with a mini-laparotomy—we're going straight to the O.R. Who told you I wanted to do a mini-laparotomy here?'

'Dr Newsome—' the nurse began, before John cut her off abruptly.

'I'm the senior resident here,' he said sharply. 'We'll take her straight to the O.R. Like right now!'

The nurse merely raised her eyebrows and gave Jan a quick, meaningful glance. John could be arrogant—everyone knew that. He was a man who liked to throw his weight around a bit, especially with those who were not in a position to answer back. Sometimes Jan wondered why she loved him.

'John.' Jan went to him and spoke to him quietly, while the X-ray technician speedily began to take abdominal and chest X-rays. 'She could be pregnant. This could be a ruptured ectopic.'

'Yeah.' That was all he said.

The boyfriend had retreated to the doorway of the small examination room, which was now crowded with the bulky X-ray machine, where he stood anxiously shifting his weight from one foot to the other. Jan went over to him.

'What the hell's going on?' He appealed to her again.

'The X-rays should give us some idea where she's bleeding from, whether it's in the chest cavity or the abdominal cavity,' she explained carefully, trying to calm him. 'We won't wait here for the X-rays to be developed—there isn't time. We'll take her to the operating rooms, and by that time the films will be ready.' As she spoke she quickly completed some rudimentary notes that she had started. The woman was beyond giving consent to any operation. Anyway, in an emergency like this, consent was not necessary.

'Tell me her name, please,' she said, 'and the address. I know she's thirty-two years old, right?'

'Yes. Her name's Cory…short for…short for… Caroline.' His pale face crumpled. Tears squeezed through his tightly shut eyelids.

'It's OK.' Jan put a comforting hand on his arm. 'Just take it easy. We're doing everything we can. Tell me her surname.'

'It's Phillips,' he said, making a supreme effort to keep his voice from breaking. 'She's Caroline Phillips.'

Jan would have reason to remember that name. In fact, she knew later that she would never forget it. Indeed, that woman, and the 'case' she represented, would teach Jan several valuable lessons—although she would often had difficulty in sorting out what exactly those lessons were. One thing she found out was that to be right, when her senior was wrong, was not always an easy situation to be in.

Jan led the woman's friend away to a seat in the corridor. The last thing he needed to witness, she figured, was one doctor, relatively young and inexperienced himself, pulling rank on another. 'You wait here for now,' she said kindly. 'You've done as much as you can. Cory's going to be taken to the operating room now. They'll find out where she's bleeding from and get it stopped. I'll tell the nurse where you are, then as soon as we have some news for you we'll call down to let you know.'

'Will she be all right?'

Trying not to flinch or hesitate as she looked at him, Jan pushed back her untidy hair from her face and stalled for time, trying to find the right words that would give him some hope yet not be an outright lie. The woman was in a bad way—there was no getting away from that fact. 'We have the staff and the expertise here in this hospital to do the best for her,' she said. 'We have a senior staff man on his way here to help with the operation.'

When Caroline Phillips passed them a few minutes later, flat on a stretcher, *en route* to the operating room, Jan squeezed the man's shoulder and left him. After making sure that the registered nurse there knew where he was, she made her way directly to the operating suite and prepared to scrub for the case.

As she stood, soaping her hands and arms, she thought of the nickname that some of the nurses in the operating rooms had given John Clairmont, unbeknown to him. He was 'Cut 'n' Gut' Clairmont, which referred to his penchant for the scalpel. He simply loved to operate at any and every available opportunity—whether it was appropriate or not.

The X-rays showed that there was a lot of blood in the chest cavity, as well as some—a lesser amount—in the abdominal cavity. By that time the patient was already on the operating table under a general anaesthetic.

'Right,' John said, 'we'll open the chest.'

Jan spoke quietly to the circulating nurse in their operating room. 'Have an abdominal laparotomy set-up on hand as well,' she said. 'I have a feeling we're going to need it.' That request gave Jan some satisfaction, after what she had perceived as a put-down of her judgement in the emergency department. Outwardly calm, she had been seething inside.

She had been weeping inside too, depressed by a premonition that what she had thought might be a beautiful romance between her and John was about to be nipped in the bud. She had been blinded, perhaps, by outward appearances.

'Sure.' The nurse smiled. 'No sweat! We can be ready for that in about sixty seconds flat. We've already got it set up on a table, covered up.'

'That's great!' Jan said, relieved.

Once they got the chest open they found the cavity awash

with fresh blood. There was a lot of activity as the surgical team suctioned and swabbed out the blood, while more dripped back into the patient's veins via the transfusion.

It took them precious minutes of exploration to discover that there was no source of bleeding within the chest cavity. The realization dawned reluctantly on John Clairmont and on the chest surgery resident, who had agreed with the decision to open the chest.

'She may have a ruptured ectopic pregnancy,' Jan ventured tentatively, but unable to keep the urgency out of her voice, 'She was lying down the whole time from the moment that she fainted. The pressure of blood in the abdominal cavity could have forced some of it up into the chest, around the esophageal opening in the diaphragm. I...er...I read about a case like that once...'

If Jan was right, one of the woman's Fallopian tubes would have ruptured from the pressure of a tubal pregnancy. It was not very often that an ovum was fertilized in the Fallopian tube, instead of in the uterus, but when it did happen the result was very often this very serious surgical emergency.

At that point the staff surgeon arrived. The circulating nurse quietly and efficiently, opened the abdominal laparotomy set of instruments. Without a word the staff man, seeing at a glance what was going on, took up a scalpel and made the appropriate cut to open the abdominal cavity.

That was the beginning of the end or perhaps, more accurately, it was the end of the beginning. The trouble was that you didn't stop loving someone overnight. Maybe what she had felt had been infatuation, fueled by a certain amount of awe that a junior doctor often felt for someone her senior. That awe had clouded her vision. What she had seen before as professional expertise had been a lack of meaningful experience, disguised by posturing—an attitude that could be dangerous to patients.

Word got around the hospital among a lot of the surgical staff that the young Dr Clairmont had made a wrong diagnosis, that a patient had almost died on the operating table and that the junior resident, Dr Jan Newsome, had been the one to urge a laparotomy, thus probably saving the patient's life. Jan knew that the staff surgeon would have done the right thing anyway, but the damage was done between herself and John.

Never one to admit to his own bad judgement, John's attitude to her changed abruptly. In his own estimation he had suffered a major loss of face, to which Jan had contributed, although in reality such things were not uncommon. He treated her as though she had done it deliberately, to do him a personal injury, whereas, in fact, she had felt sick with fear at the time that Caroline Phillips would not survive.

If only he had listened to the judgements of all members of his team in the first place, the outcome might have been different. In any event, he made life very difficult for her on the surgical team afterwards. It was John's father, Roderick Clairmont, who suggested that John transferred to another city teaching hospital to finish the short period of post-grad training in surgery that he had left to complete. So he had gone, leaving her with a loss of faith in her judgement of men. The rest, as they say, was history.

Muffled voices came to her, those of her father and Gerard de Prescy, bringing her thoughts back to the present and St Bonar. Getting up, she dressed quickly in a pair of cotton trousers and a loose top.

The men were standing at the front of the house with the horse when she went down the steps in the half-light of early morning. They turned to look at her.

Dawn came up quickly on St Bonar. Already the cool light was tinged with yellow. A stiff breeze rustled the tops of the coconut palms that edged the lawn at the side of the house.

'Good morning,' Jan said. 'You're leaving, Dr de Prescy?' For her father's sake, she did not want more of an atmosphere between them than there was already. And he *had* helped her to arrive safely...

'Call me Gerard,' he said, unfazed by any vibes. 'Yes, I'm leaving.'

With one arm casually on the saddle of the horse as he stood beside it, he looked very different. He had obviously borrowed some clothes from her father—a short-sleeved shirt, too small to button over his broad chest, and some cotton pants that were rolled up to below the knees. Seeing her scrutiny, he grinned slightly.

'Beggars can't be choosers,' he said.

Jan smiled, in spite of her still seething sense of outrage.

'You do look rather like a beggar in that outfit,' she agreed. But attractive, nonetheless, she had to concede. His hair, clean now, was damp and brushed back from his face.

'How are you going to get out of here?' she enquired.

'Your father's going to show me a better way out,' he said, fixing her with his dark gaze. 'He's going to point me in the right direction.'

'Morning, Jan,' her father said. 'I'm just going to drive ahead of Gerard a short distance and show him a way out. You help yourself to coffee, and there's plenty of food.'

'Thanks, Dad. Um...' Jan turned to the other man. 'I want to thank you for coming with me yesterday. I know I may have appeared less than grateful at the time.' There were a few seconds of charged tension, a forced politeness, between them as Jan recalled—and no doubt he did too— how they had lain together under the trees. 'I'm afraid I've taken up rather a lot of your time.'

'My pleasure,' Gerard said softly, his deep voice barely audible. His gaze rested on her mouth, managing to let her know that he was also referring to that kiss. 'I couldn't let Jack Newsome's daughter get lost, could I?' There was a touch of irony in his words. Not for a moment could she forget that he also had other motives for being there.

She let his remark pass. 'I hope to work while I'm here,' she said, changing tack. 'I've asked Dr Don McLean to give me a temporary job.'

'You know Dr McLean personally?' he asked. Dr McLean also acted as the chief medical officer on the island, and had been there for over twenty years.

'Yes. I telephoned when I knew I was coming. Before the storm, fortunately,' she confirmed, managing to let him know by the tone of her voice that she knew the island pretty well, together with the long-established personnel in the medical profession.

'There's plenty of work at the moment,' he said noncommittally, 'while this mess gets cleared up so maybe we'll meet again after all, Janine, before you return to the States. When is Don planning to let you know what you'll be needed for?'

'As soon as I get in touch with him by phone, I should imagine,' she said.

'The telephones are still functioning in Fletchette,' he said, referring to a small village nearby, 'if you can make your way through to there.'

Jan remembered the village on the other side of the landslide, which they should be able to reach along the lane from Manara once it had been cleared of superficial debris. There was a local bar—a rum shop—in the village which had a public telephone on its verandah.

'Good,' she said.

She watched him mount the big horse with ease, and watched her father start up the Land Rover and drive ahead slowly up the slight incline of the lane, that led away from the house.

'Goodbye, Janine.'

'Goodbye. Hope you get through without too much trouble.' Jan sat down on the stone steps to see them off, letting out a long breath of relief. At the bend in the lane, which would take him from her view, the doctor turned in the saddle to give her a quick casual salute.

With her elbows propped on her knees, Jan cupped her face pensively with her hands, watching the sun come up. Well, here she was! Ready at last to really find out what was what in this place. It was evident that her father was ill—that much she knew already. What to do about it was the question. He accused her of being stubborn, yet he himself was more so in his quiet way.

From somewhere in the distance a cock was crowing faintly, heralding the beginning of the working day to those who wanted to make the best of the few cool hours before the relentless sun reached far into the sky. Already the mourning doves that lived in the garden were starting up their plaintive, poignant calling.

The flowers themselves had no scent, yet the earth around gave off the pungence of fertility. Jan sighed, drinking in with all her senses the vista before her. There was a strong feeling that a chapter in her life had ended, and another was about to begin.

Back in the quiet house she poured herself a mug of coffee in the big, old-fashioned kitchen, then wandered, coffee-mug in hand, through the spacious sitting room, furnished with old mahogany and rattan furniture, into the room off it which served as a library and a study-cum-office for her father. She looked around her vaguely, hoping that perhaps she might see evidence of the financial demise of their estate among the untidy files. At the desk, littered with papers and letters, Jan idly shifted a few items here and there with one hand as she sipped her coffee.

A name on an open sheet of paper seemed to jump out

at her, causing her heart to give an uncomfortable lurch. It was the name Clairmont. Gingerly she picked up the piece of paper, recalling Gerard de Prescy's words that her father had a list of possible surgeons who might want to come to St Bonar for short periods and who might want to look at the house. Hardly daring to breathe, as though the hand of fate had touched her in this remote place, she scanned the typed names. Halfway down was the name 'R. Clairmont,' with the appellation 'plastic surgeon'.

She let out a breath. Not John, then. It was his father. Thank God…not John.

CHAPTER FOUR

SO THIS was the clinic. Jan leaned forward over the steering wheel of her father's Land Rover to get a better look as she eased the vehicle up the last part of the uneven dirt lane which, she could see, came to a dead end behind the flat-roofed, white-painted, brick and concrete building that was the Eden Bay clinic.

A narrow street had twisted and turned up a hillside, before turning into a lane. As she had negotiated the road she had caught glimpses from time to time of the spectacular view back down to the coast to the brilliant blue of the ocean. The village, clinging to the side of the hill, was liberally endowed with brilliant climbing, flowering shrubs. As a child, she had never come up this far. She parked the Land Rover under the shade of a spreading calabash tree and got out.

All was quiet and peaceful—no one about. A breeze blew in from the sea, tempering the heat. The ground where she stood was dry, the grass a golden brown. A week had gone by since the day of her arrival, and this was the first day of her job on St Bonar, which she had confirmed with the chief medical officer. The unpaved road into Manara had been cleared during the past week and a temporary bypass road bulldozed out on Manara property to go around the landslide on the main road so that they could get to Fort Roche. The telephones were still not reliable.

Don McLean, the chief medical officer, had said he would meet her here to go over the routine with her, but there was no sign of him. Jan tried the door to the clinic. It was locked. The building was small and squat, standing

on its own generous plot of land and amply shaded by
mature trees in the center of the Eden Bay community yet
away from the bustle of the market area lower down. This
was a quiet residential place.

Bougainvillea was shedding its brilliant petals liberally
on the dry, sun-baked earth. There was no obvious storm
damage here or evidence of heavy rain, apart from that
coloured carpet. The solid walls of the single-story clinic
were intact, as was its roof. The small windows were barred
like a prison.

Since her first morning at Manara Jan had not set eyes
on Dr Gerard, as he liked to be called. At the moment she
had no idea how large he would loom in her life here. It
would be great to be more or less her own boss for a
change, even though she would be part of a co-ordinated
team that worked to serve the island. After the noise and
rush of a city, the peace was gradually having a therapeutic
effect. The last thing she wanted was someone supervising
her every move—she would feel she was not of much real
use.

Jan sat down on a simple plank bench under the tree.
She would stay on St Bonar for however long it took for
her father to get well and to sort out his immediate affairs,
which tied in so closely with her own. One of the things
she would make quite sure of was that Dr Gerard would
not relieve them of their property if some other solution to
their money problems could be found, even if it meant that
her father retired and she took on the property herself, with
the very able help of the manager and staff.

It was doubtful that her father was really well, in spite
of his protestations to that effect now that she was here in
the flesh. The breath test that she had done for the *Helicobacter pylori* had proved positive. Now she had to arrange for a few more tests before she started him on the

medication she had brought with her. Don McLean had confirmed that he would take him on.

For the first time in ages Jan felt free and happy, enjoying the feel of the warm breeze rippling the short blue and white floral skirt that she wore with a white sleeveless blouse. She wriggled her bare toes appreciatively in the open sandals that lightly encased her feet. Her soft blonde hair, newly washed that morning, was pulled back from her face with a ribbon in a loose ponytail. It made her feel young and carefree...almost. Memories of snow, blizzards and slush were rapidly receding from her mind.

There was the sound of a car grinding up the side of the steep hill. Maybe that would be Don McLean, whom she had not yet actually seen on this visit to the island. When a small, blue, battered car made its appearance in the lane and drove towards her, Jan stood up in anticipation.

At the wheel was not the fifty-five-year old Don McLean, but Gerard de Prescy. As Jan stared with something like dismay he stopped the car and got out, easing his large frame through the door that seemed inadequate for him.

'Hi!' he called. 'Been waiting long?'

Oh, hell! Why did it have to be him? Jan spoke the words to herself, feeling tense. At the same time she felt a frisson of anticipation. 'No, about ten minutes,' she called back.

Taking off his sunglasses, he slowly walked towards her. His eyes roamed over her, from her neat hair down to her feet in the trim white sandals. 'So, we meet again, Miss Newsome,' he said. 'I hope this is not too disagreeable for you.'

Jan was conscious of looking very different from when he had first set eyes on her. The sun had put some colour in her cheeks too.

She merely smiled, wary of his motives.

'Don McLean couldn't make it,' he said, the slight West

Indian accent striking her anew. 'He asked me to come instead.'

Jan nodded, saying nothing. Like her, he certainly looked different. The somewhat elemental man of the previous week had become more sophisticated in the interim, yet he was dressed for the climate and for work. The simple loose linen trousers that he wore, together with the striped blue and white open-neck shirt, enhanced his overt masculinity. His hair, which still curled a little over his forehead, had been cut short.

'How are you?' he asked unsmilingly, the slight formality of those words vying with the warm lilt of his voice.

'I'm fine,' she said, a nervous tightness in her throat. 'Looking forward to getting to work.'

'And your father?'

'He seems all right so far. The test was positive for the bacteria,' Jan said, very conscious of his presence. How she wished he were Dr McLean.

'That's a start,' he said. 'Have you persuaded him to take the other tests? Maybe I could be of some help there.'

'Thank you. I may have to take you up on that. Nothing's settled yet.' Jan felt her earlier carefree mood being replaced by a tenseness that she could not identify. This man appeared very at ease with his masculinity so that he took it entirely for granted, unlike some of the men she had worked with who capitalized like mad on any good looks they had. That had always put her somewhat on the defensive. His lack of what she called 'attitude', which she normally found refreshing, left her momentarily nonplussed.

'What have you got planned?' he asked.

'Well…' She tried to gather her jumbled thoughts. 'He's more or less agreed that the tests are necessary, but I know he'll just let it slide. I'll have to make all the appointments and make sure that he keeps them.' She squinted up at him.

'All he cares about when he's here is the estate. But he did ask me to come...'

'Hmm...' Gerard said thoughtfully, looking at her with a frown. 'Maybe you should start him on the antibiotics anyway. Don't wait for the other tests.'

'Yes. I was thinking maybe I should do that.'

Jangling a bunch of keys absently in his hand, he turned from her to look at the clinic building. 'The Eden Bay clinic is new since you were last here, I guess,' he commented. 'It's one of several new freestanding clinics on the island now so that patients can go to the one nearest where they live, instead of making the long trek to Fort Roche. We— the doctors—have a roster for staffing these places, together with the nurses. We try to keep some sort of continuity of care, particularly with the obstetrics cases and the children.'

'I see,' she said, aware that she sounded stiff and unnatural. At least they were on safe ground, talking about work. 'That seems like a great arrangement. It's a good thing something's new. There hasn't been much new since the end of colonial days.'

'Quite,' he said. 'The hospital's pretty old—the one in Fort Roche—quite run-down in some places. That's why we need a new place for our private patients.'

'At Manara?' Jan said.

'Possibly...possibly not. It is rather far from the town, the airport and other facilities.'

'It's also a private house. It's part of the history of this island.'

'It's also a house that not many·people could afford to keep up. We can still preserve history,' he said, looking at her shrewdly. 'I'm the last person to want to destroy a beautiful house.'

'I prefer not to discuss it now,' she said pointedly, moving towards the clinic building.

The nod he gave her was one of acquiescence. 'As you

wish. You have some obstetrics training, I understand?' he queried, as he walked beside her. 'You mentioned it when we met. As well as general surgery, your main specialty, and pediatrics?'

'Yes. I settled on general surgery,' Jan said.

'All those things will be extremely useful here,' he said. 'Just what's needed.' Jan felt that he was making an effort to be agreeable to her. 'You won't want to stay on St Bonar long, I assume?'

'Well…no. I'll stay as long as necessary. I have three months' leave,' she said.

It was a relief that they were now talking strictly business. She and her father had not yet had time to come up with any feasible alternatives to this man's offer to buy their estate. They had been too busy considering the implications of the storm, trying to manage without staff and worrying about the physical symptoms that had been plaguing her father for some time.

He began to sort through keys. 'Shall we go in?' he said, moving ahead of her. The door had two locks of a type difficult to force. 'Looks like Fort Knox, doesn't it?' he added drily.

'Yes.' She smiled as he juggled keys. 'Is that necessary?'

'Unfortunately, yes. Crime here is mainly of a petty nature, but it's nonetheless there.'

'Are you a general surgeon?' she asked.

'Yes, although I have some training in plastic surgery. That's a big interest of mine so I manage to deal with some of the birth defects that occur here in babies—cleft palates, that sort of thing. I function as a GP as well…a bit of everything.' He deftly fitted keys. 'I did my undergraduate training in the UK, then some of my post-graduate work in the States as I have dual citizenship through my parents. I was born on Martinique. My grandfather, and now my father, have had property there for a long time.'

'I see. A man with a foot in many camps.' Jan found that she was trying not to like him, not to feel the pull of his sexual attraction, but was finding it an uphill battle.

She did not want a quick affair, over in three months, in time for her to resume her usual life. Besides, for all she knew, he might be married, with a brood of children...although there had been no hint of that. It was hardly a question she could ask him now.

'The young kids still get kwashiorkor here, the African disease of malnutrition. Did you know that?' he informed her.

'Well, I knew they got it in the past,' she said slowly, surprised by his news. 'I thought the situation would have improved by now.'

'No. There's still a lot to be done about child care, and preventative care for women, too. We're trying to set up an island-wide program for cervical screening for the women to make sure that every woman of a certain age gets a pap smear once a year,' he said. 'There's an awful lot of cervical cancer here. By the time we get to see it it's quite often inoperable.'

'I hadn't realized it was so bad,' Jan said soberly, impressed with his professional commitment, in spite of her uncertainty about him personally. It was still difficult for her to think of Gerard as a doctor and not some sort of property developer. Of course, he wanted to be both, she reminded herself, with Manara as the starting point.

'The way it is now, they have to get into Fort Roche for their pap smears. As you can imagine, a lot of them don't bother—it's just too much of an effort when they have young children.'

'It's a familiar story,' Jan commented.

'It's a great tragedy when a mother dies...anywhere. It seems even more so here,' he said, pushing open the metal door. 'Leaving young kids. Mothers are very often the center of the family here, together with grandmothers. They're often the main breadwinners as well. They hold everything together.'

'Yes,' she said.

'One of our first priorities is to get that program started for the women,' he went on, 'and a better birth-control program. We need healthier babies and fewer of them, who survive childhood without these debilitating diseases associated with malnutrition. These clinics are the first part of that solution.'

He spoke passionately and, surprising herself, Jan felt her antipathy fraying at the edges as she agreed with every word he said, feeling the excitement of the professional challenge. She could not fault him.

'In a place like this,' he went on, 'a lack of money produces apathy. Quite often it's one step forward and two steps back, if you're not careful.'

'Do you do routine tests for the human papilloma virus on the women as well when they come for their pap tests?' she asked, referring to the cervical screening test that could detect a pre-cancerous condition that, if left untreated, could lead to cancer of the cervix. She knew that the HPV test picked up high-grade abnormalities of the cervical cells which were not picked up by the other routine smear test.

'So far we haven't done it,' he said. 'That's one of the things we want to start as soon as possible. It's mainly through a lack of money that we haven't done it. We have to get people to come to St Bonar to train our lab technicians to process the tests, as well as show our doctors and nurses how to do the tests. Then, of course, we have to get the programs in place in the clinics.'

'That's something I could do,' Jan said, tuning in to his sense of urgency, his enthusiasm. 'I know how to do those tests, and the lab work.'

'You do?' He looked at her consideringly. 'That's great!

Maybe you're going to be an asset to us, after all, Dr Newsome.' There was a touch of humor in his voice.

'I believe I am,' she said.

'Maybe we could set up a quick training program for the nurses while you're here,' he said. 'They take a lot of the pap smears.'

'I'd be glad to do it,' Jan said eagerly, gratified that already her presence on the island promised to be of some very practical use. 'There's a fair amount of tuberculosis here, too, so I understand?'

'Yes, in both children and adults. There's quite a lot of AIDS as well,' he said.

If he felt the same degree of underlying awkwardness that she felt about their first encounter, Jan thought as she followed him closely into the dim, hot, interior of the clinic, he certainly didn't show it. For all his natural ease there was a subtle reticence about him that had, most likely, nothing to do with her—she had noticed it before. Probably it was perfectly natural for him to kiss a woman when he found himself lying on top of her. Jan grinned to herself, remembering.

She wondered whether he was as determined to buy their family estate as she was to hang on to it. If so, there was definitely going to be a battle. She just hoped that she had enough time to wage it. Her mother and brother in England would have something to say about it, although she suspected that her mother, weary of the responsibility, might be only too happy to let it go. Her brother, born too late to feature in her grandfather's will, also loved the place.

'There's been no one here for a while,' Gerard said, as he flicked on switches to start up ceiling fans which immediately shifted the stagnant air. Then he opened shutters to reveal to Jan the stark, utilitarian interior. 'All the trauma cases resulting from the storm went down to Fort Roche, together with whatever staff we have here, which isn't much. We have a registered nurse here part time. Her name's Anne. I'm here as often as I can be.'

'I see.'

'Take a look around, Janine,' he offered, 'and call me Gerard. There's little formality here.'

Jan shrugged. 'All right, Gerard,' she agreed a little stiffly, still determined not to let down her guard. 'Do you approve of me being here? Having a job that has to be paid for?'

It was his turn to shrug. 'As I said, you'll be a great asset. It does seem a bit of a waste of time for those who have to orientate you for only three months,' he conceded. 'Not that we don't appreciate all the help we can get in this crisis.'

There was something in his tone that made her feel as though he thought her a dilettante, just passing through, able to get a job because of her acquaintance with Don McLean.

'I intend to work hard,' she announced, not flinching from his direct gaze. 'And—as you must know—we need the money. I'm not in the habit of getting a free ride…anywhere.' Her annoyance came through in her tone as she stared at him so he put up his hands in a conciliatory gesture.

'Fair enough,' he said. 'Talking of money, there's certainly not enough for the luxury of disposable equipment here.' His eyes followed her glance around the reception area. It was clean, bright and utilitarian in the extreme. 'It's a mixed blessing, anyway. Costs become astronomical very quickly, then there's the problem of how and where to dispose of plastics and such things. On St Bonar all used equipment is carefully cleaned and resterilized for future use.'

Jan nodded. Don McLean must have given him instructions to give her a very thorough orientation, she decided as she followed him on a tour of several small treatment rooms and the trauma area, where there was an anesthetic machine and intravenous equipment. From what she could see, the clinic was sparsely but adequately equipped. A preparation room contained a small autoclave for sterilizing instruments and other equipment by hot steam under pressure.

'Where do you do your operating?' she asked, determined to be unfazed by whatever he might say to her.

'I'm at the Royal Hospital in Fort Roche a lot of the time. I have no set operating days,' he said. 'I also go to four other clinics in more rural areas, where I sometimes do very minor surgery under local anaesthetic.'

From now on this clinic would be her province until further notice, Jan assumed. It was a job that had been given to her with surprising trust by the authorities. Although she was well known on the island, they had no idea what sort of a doctor she was—whether she was good, mediocre or downright bad. Looking around her at the basic facilities, probably the very best that the poverty-stricken island could offer its people, she renewed her resolve to do her utmost to be of real use to justify their trust in her.

'That's about it,' Gerard said, when she had explored every part of the clinic. 'Would you like a cup of good coffee? Or maybe a cold drink? I brought a cooler full of stuff with me to put in the fridge. There's an electric kettle around here somewhere that we can use as the power is obviously functioning.'

'I'd appreciate some coffee,' Jan smiled. 'Thanks.'

'Good. You find the kettle. I'll get the stuff from my car.'

The kettle was in a cupboard under a sink. In a matter of minutes her colleague had made delicious coffee for them. 'This is Jamaican,' he said, handing her a mug. 'Blue Mountain coffee.'

'Mmm... It smells wonderful. Thank you.' For a moment their eyes met, his dark and quizzical. Oddly, meeting his look, Jan momentarily felt herself to be out of place, a foreigner who did not belong here—she who had prided herself on being a child of the islands, very much a part of this one.

'I hope you brought plenty of good insect repellent with you,' he said, staring out of the small window in front of them, which had an insect screen on it as well as the bars. 'I heard two days ago that there's an outbreak of dengue fever in Trinidad. We're trying to control travel to and from there, but it's difficult.'

'That's all you need!' Jan said commiseratingly. 'Yes, I did bring repellent. It's the mosquito that spreads it, after biting an infected person, isn't it?'

'That's right, so we have to try to keep the infected people out, of course. Easier said than done, if they don't know they're incubating it. It's the *Aëdes aegypti* mosquito.' Again he looked at her, at her bare arms and legs. 'You need to wear long sleeves and pants. That should help to protect you if there's an outbreak.'

'Um...they've had outbreaks in Mexico and Texas,' she said, very aware of his open appraisal. They were standing close to each other and she did not want to be the first one to move away in case he should see her as being as uptight as she felt. Work stress had taken its toll on her, she could see that now. Maybe in another two weeks of this life she could really relax. 'I have to admit, though, that I don't know as much about it as I should.'

'It used to be called "breakbone fever",' he explained, between sips of coffee, 'because of the severe pains in the joints and muscles. People who've got it get a high fever, which comes on abruptly. There's loss of appetite, followed by nausea and vomiting. Then there's a measles-like rash over the chest and arms. You can't mistake it once you know it's about.'

'It's a virus, isn't it?' Jan ventured, trying to think of all she had heard and read about the disease. 'And there's a hemorrhagic variety that can be very serious, I think.'

'Right on both counts,' he said. 'Something not to be taken lightly. One of the important things in treatment is not to prescribe any aspirin in the hemorrhagic variety as that can increase the possibility of bleeding.'

'You're beginning to have me worried,' Jan ventured with a smile, trying to lighten the atmosphere. 'I guess I'll get some sort of warning from other members of the medical team if they think it's managed to arrive here.'

'Yes, we all keep in close touch about such things. What makes it rather difficult to deal with is that there are four types of the dengue virus,' he said.

'Meaning that someone who's had it once or twice before can still get it again from a different virus?'

'That's right,' he said. 'Let me pour you some more coffee.'

'Thanks,' Jan handed over her cup. 'Some of my male colleagues in Boston would never get me coffee so this is nice. There, it's every woman for herself.'

'I know what you mean,' he said, adding milk to her mug of coffee. 'Here you're a human being first, a woman or man second.' He handed over the mug. 'Not that a man doesn't thoroughly appreciate a beautiful woman.' This time his eyes explored her face, taking in every feature carefully. 'Especially one who can blush so sweetly.'

'I…' Jan found herself at a loss for words.

'Don't apologize,' he said softly. 'It *is* sweet. And not to be taken as a sign of weakness. Sorry… I shouldn't have put you on the spot like that.' He was smiling at her, a gesture that softened his rather craggy features, making him surprisingly more attractive.

'It's all right. I'm a little on the defensive. It'll pass.'

'What happened between us in the woods was just one of those things,' he said candidly.

'Yes, I know. You must think I'm an idiot,' she blurted out. 'It's just that for the past months I've sort of tried to tune out the male sex somewhat—except in a strictly professional way.' The men she had dallied with after John did not seem to count.

'Why?' he said bluntly.

'Oh...' Jan hesitated, not wanting to go into the old once-bitten-twice-shy routine. 'Let me just say that I had a clash between the very personal and the professional, in which the personal did not come off well.'

'Hmm...' he murmured. 'I think I know what you mean. Sounds like a variation on a fairly common theme.'

Jan bit her lip, keeping her eyes focused on the floor, willing the color in her cheeks to subside. Now why the hell did I tell him that? she admonished herself. 'It may be common, but not easy to deal with,' she said.

'I didn't mean to imply that it was,' he said softly, in such a way that Jan picked up the nuances that implied much in his own background. She wondered again if he had a family...if he was married.

In spite of a heightened awareness between them, Jan felt that the atmosphere had lightened—changed—so that a certain subtle understanding had been arrived at. She found herself giving an inward sigh of relief. Yet at the same time her intuition hinted to her that the relief was premature. There was no way that she wanted to relax her guard.

'Do you usually feel that a personal admission is a sign of weakness, Janine?'

The question took Jan by surprise. 'I'm not sure,' she said, looking at him quickly to find him watching her. 'Quite often the person you are telling it to takes it as such...so I have found.'

'Hmm.'

He moved over to the sink in the tiny kitchen area off the reception room where she was standing, and proceeded to wash the items they had used. Thankfully, he did not pursue that issue.

'Will you be leaving me to it now?' she asked.

'I'll hang around for a while,' Gerard said, his back to her, 'just in case there's a deluge of patients. The people around here know my car. They may at this moment be toiling up the hill.'

Jan began again to look in cupboards to see what drugs and other supplies they had on hand, trying to memorize exactly where everything of importance was kept. From time to time she made notes in the notebook she had brought with her.

CHAPTER FIVE

'HELLO!' A man's voice called from the doorway, breaking into the pleasant, warm silence of the clinic. 'Dr Gerard! Are you there?'

'Looks like we've got a patient,' Gerard said. He had been going through files in the office area where they also kept the narcotics cupboard which Jan had been exploring. He stood up. 'We'll have to put further exploration on hold. News travels fast in this place.'

'Dr Gerard!' the voice persisted.

'We're here!' Gerard called out. From a cupboard in the office he took out two clean lab coats and handed one to Jan. 'Here, put this on.'

Out in the reception area they were confronted by a middle-aged local man, who was standing in the open doorway, leaning on a pair of crude home-made crutches. A battered felt hat covered his head above a very weathered face, and his clothes had seen better days. The foot he was standing on was bare. The other, which he held up behind him, was covered with a cloth tied on with string. There hung about him a smell of putrefaction.

'Dr Gerard,' the man's face creased in a relieved smile, showing several gaps in his teeth. 'I bin waiting. Saw your car come up, so I thought now's my chance. Got a bad foot. Poisoned. Can't hardly walk.'

'I can see that you have.' Gerard shook hands with the man, who wobbled dangerously on his crutches. 'What do you expect when you go around without shoes? Come in.' The smile he gave the man tempered the implied admonition in his words.

'Shoes fell to bits in the rain,' the man explained, wielding the crutches expertly as he entered the clinic. 'Can't mend 'em, can't afford to buy more.'

'It's Etienne, isn't it? I've seen you before.'

'*Oui*, Dr Gerard, that's me.'

'Get up here, man.' Gerard helped their patient up onto the table in one of the treatment rooms, while Jan hung back, preferring to be an observer for now. 'Does the foot hurt a lot?'

'It hurt like hell, man. Can't stand it. Rum don't keep it away neither.'

As Gerard put on a pair of rubber gloves and gently cut the string around the foot and unwrapped the cloth, the two men engaged in a rapid conversation in the local patois that was a mixture of French and English, another legacy from the island's mixed colonial past. It was good to hear it again, and Jan found herself grinning at the odd mixture of words which had a very practical utility.

'Etienne's a fisherman, here in Eden Bay.' Gerard turned to Jan, including her in the conversation. 'Did you understand what he was saying?'

'More or less. He trod on a sharp piece of wood during the rains, which went right through his shoe. Right?'

'Right.' Gerard eased off one of the rubber gloves and put a hand on her arm to draw her forward, 'Etienne, this is Dr Newsome, the daughter of Mr Newsome at Manara. She's going to be working here for a few weeks, helping us out.'

'Eh! Eh!' Etienne exclaimed, lifting up his head to get a better look at her. 'She look too young to be a doctor.'

'Hi. Pleased to meet you.' Jan smiled. The hand lingered on her bare arm.

'She may look young, but she's very well qualified,' Gerard said, looking at her sideways, perhaps to let her know that he was quite capable of giving compliments, as he slid his warm hand from her arm and put the glove back on.

The foot was grossly swollen. Close up, Jan could smell the infection even more, a sickly, pervasive odour. A few flies, which must have come in when they opened the screen door, buzzed and hovered over it. They could see a dark puncture wound, oozing pus, in the sole of the foot where the stick had entered.

'We'll fix you up, Etienne,' Gerard said, manipulating the foot gently while the man winced with pain. 'We may have to transfer you later to the Royal Hospital for more treatment. You're lucky you haven't got gas gangrene, man. You shouldn't have let it go so long.'

'Eh! Eh! Oh, Lordy! Lordy! You mean dat, Dr Gerard? The old woman won't want me go down there!' Etienne exclaimed, his face contorting with anguish.

'I'm afraid I do mean it,' Gerard said sternly. 'You neglect yourself like that, you have to pay the consequences. A lot of people have to have a leg amputated with a foot like that. You're lucky you're not dead.'

'But I wait for you,' the man protested again. 'I wait for you three days! Only today you come. Oh, the good Lord have mercy!'

'I've been busy elsewhere. I'm only here now to show the clinic to Dr Newsome. Now we've got to get to work on this pretty quick.'

While their patient again launched into a stream of the local lingo, explaining the nature of his injury again and the reasons for his delay in seeking help, Gerard stripped off the rubber gloves, put them into a bucket and filled it with water and disinfectant. Then he put on a cotton face mask and handed one to her.

'We use our gloves again,' he said to Jan, who was silently watching him. 'We even put patches on them when they get holes, just like the old days.' As he soaped his hands at the sink he nodded towards several plastic aprons that were hanging on a hook. 'Put one of those on. You're going to need it.'

'I can see that,' she agreed, smiling. The small room was filled with an almost unbearable odor.

'Zap those flies with that spray over there, would you, Jan?' Gerard said. 'Then get your hands scrubbed and put on a pair of gloves.'

As Jan did as she was instructed, Gerard opened up equipment and swiftly took the patient's temperature, pulse rate and blood pressure. 'I'm going to put up an intravenous line first,' he said, 'and give him some dextrose and saline. He's got fever and a rip-roaring infection in that foot. I guess I don't have to tell you that—you can go by the smell. So, tell me, Dr Newsome, how would you treat this case?' He used her title for the benefit of the patient.

While he quickly prepared an intravenous line and a bag of fluid, he waited for her reply.

'Um…' Jan cleared her throat. If he wanted to quiz her as though she were a third year-medical student, then she would go along with it. After all, he knew very little about her. Fighting down persistent niggles of irritation, she proceeded to explain her campaign of treatment. 'Well, I agree with what you are doing right now. I would give him plenty of I.V. fluids, plus a large I.V. bolus of a broad-spectrum antibiotic, stat, to be followed by intramuscular antibiotics every four hours…or maybe continue them I.V. if the fever persists. I would then give him intravenous sedation, plus some local anaesthetic to the foot, then I would tackle the foot.'

'Good. Go on.' He had the bag of intravenous fluid hanging up on a pole and was now flushing the attached plastic I.V. line with the fluid. As she proceeded to talk he started to insert an I.V. cannula into a vein in the back of Etienne's hand, gently explaining to him what he was about to do.

'I would clean up the foot with a soap solution on the outside initially, followed by an iodine-based solution, then I would irrigate the puncture wound with copious amounts of hydrogen peroxide. With any puncture wound there is, I know, the possibility of gas gangrene—'

'Caused by?'

'Caused by the bacterium *Clostridium welchii*, type A, of course,' she said crisply. It was an anaerobic bacterium, one capable of surviving without oxygen, that thrived in areas of the body and in wounds where no oxygen could reach. Jan paused, wondering whether Etienne realized the seriousness of the condition they were talking about, whether he had ever heard of it and whether he knew how quickly it could take hold and spread.

'And...?' Gerard queried, hooking up the cannula to the plastic I.V. tubing, his large, rough hands looking incongruously gentle. Yes, Jan mused, he was definitely a doctor, not a developer, not a bricklayer, or whatever... He straightened, dwarfing her by his size in the cramped space, and shot her a quizzical look. 'Is that all, Dr Newsome?'

'No. I would open up the wound a bit, do a debridement, flush out the pus and muck and put in several rubber drains so that he could have frequent irrigation. Preferably, one would give the antibiotics longer to work, before tampering with an infected wound, but in this case, since we're giving him the bolus and because of the massive infection, I don't think we can wait very long. We've got to get it flushed out.'

'Yes, I agree. What else?'

'I agree with you that he ought to go to the Royal Hospital. He's going to need the I.V. fluid and antibiotics for about ten days, although I think that if he were going to get gas gangrene, he would have developed it by now...' Her voice trailed off. 'Um...I've never actually seen a case of it...I know there's a particular smell.'

'You're quite right,' Gerard said, adding sterile water to vials of powdered antibiotic with a syringe and hypodermic needle. 'I don't think he's got it, but we won't take any chances. We'll take several culture swabs as we go along for the bacteriology lab in Fort Roche to find out exactly what he's got growing in there.'

In moments the antibiotic was dripping from an additional fifty-milliliter bag of intravenous fluid into the patient's vein. It was always a relief, Jan mused as she watched the fluid dripping through the measuring drip chamber, to see it beginning to do its vital work of turning the tide of massive infection. She watched Gerard's skilled fingers adjusting the rate of flow.

'Shall we wait a bit,' Jan suggested, 'for at least part of the dose of antibiotics to run in before we start on the foot?' Occasionally, someone was allergic to a particular antibiotic.

'Yes, we'll wait about twenty minutes before we do anything vigorous with it. We can start to clean it up on the outside with Cetavlon and Phisohex. Would you like to do that part, Dr Newsome?'

'Yes.'

'Put on protective goggles and two pairs of gloves,' he ordered, as though she had never before done anything of this nature. Jan bit her lip, keeping her expression neutral. 'Maybe you could give him the intramuscular tetanus shot first. I've got the stuff out there on the counter. I want to give him the narcotic, I.V., before we start on the foot. This is going to be pretty painful.'

'Sure,' Jan said.

'I got pain now, man,' their patient added to the consultation, opening his eyes wearily. 'Plenty pain. *Mal, mal, mal!*'

'We're taking action right now, Etienne,' Gerard said. There was a warmth to his voice, as though he enjoyed sparring with these local men, enjoyed their humor and wit, their stoicism in adversity. That, at least, was something she had in common with this complex man.

'You're getting a painkiller,' he was saying to their patient. 'It's going to shut your tongue up too.'

'Ah, you're a hard man, Dr Gerard,' their patient murmured, closing his eyes in resignation. 'A hard, hard man. You influencing this young woman in bad ways.'

Gerard laughed softly. 'Just to prove that I'm not hard,' he said, 'I'll be the one to tell your wife that you have to go to hospital. How's that?'

'I take back all I said, man,' Etienne exclaimed, his speech becoming slurred as the narcotic began to take effect. 'I take back all I said. You married yourself, man?'

Jan kept her eyes lowered as she sensed a hesitation in her colleague before he answered. 'Not any more,' he said. 'I take my pleasure where I find it.'

Etienne laughed drily. 'That the best way.'

'Maybe...'

Jan flushed at his words.

'How...you planning to get me to the hospital?' Etienne articulated the words slowly, fighting sleep.

'We'll figure out a way,' Gerard said.

When their patient was sleeping he turned to Jan. 'I didn't mean to be dictatorial,' he said. 'I just want to get some idea of what you're familiar with in a practical sense, not just in theory. A lot of doctors never actually see these infections that they learn about from textbooks in medical school. On this island you'll see just about everything—often in its most rabid form.'

'Hmm...' Jan felt some of her irritation subsiding. 'I know you're right. Shall I prepare the instruments?'

Another question in her mind was whether he considered her a 'found' pleasure. This time of closeness was going to be difficult to get through unless she could lose herself in work.

'Do you think you can cope with this clinic? You may be here by yourself some of the time, maybe sometimes with one of our nurses.' Gerard asked the question later as they bent over the patient's malodorous foot, with a tray of sterile instruments and dressings between them. 'You'll have to clean and sterilize the instruments yourself, pack sterile trays and make sure the inventory is up to date when the nurse isn't here. We have to go into Fort Roche to get supplies from the hospital.'

Jan, suitably protected with goggles and a mask on her face, plus sterile gown and gloves, had a plastic irrigation tube deep in the wound. With a 50 cc syringe of hydrogen peroxide, she was repeatedly flushing the puncture hole. Bloody fluid came back out, flowing into a kidney dish, which her colleague held with one hand while he flexed the foot with his other hand so that Jan could see what she was doing. Etienne snored, a rubber airway in his mouth to keep his throat open.

Jan shrugged philosophically. 'Phew!' she let out the breath which she had been holding. 'I'm concentrating on trying to ignore that smell!'

'Better get used to it.' The soft laugh of commiseration that he gave was so unlike the sarcastic comments some of her usual colleagues would have given on such an admission that Jan reluctantly felt herself unbending more, as though he were drawing her emotionally closer.

'I think I can cope here. Nothing to it!' She allowed herself a slight smile, relaxed somewhat now, although still feeling that he was assessing her. He had every right to do so, she conceded reluctantly. As far as he was concerned, she was an unknown quantity.

'Tomorrow I plan to arrive early,' she said, busily filling

the syringe with more irrigation fluid, 'in the cool of the morning, well before opening time at ten o'clock, to take an inventory of all equipment and medicines that are stocked here. I want to be absolutely ready for any eventuality, to know exactly what I have on hand.'

'Mmm...' her colleague said. In the confined space of the room he loomed large. Jan was aware of vibes between them that she could not place. It was not at all clear yet what he thought of her as a medical colleague, although she was coming round to the idea that he approved.

'Is that enough irrigation now, do you think?' Jan asked. 'The fluid coming back is much clearer. I'd like to put in three of the rubber drains and make another incision to get to the base of the wound—let in some more fluid by a different route.'

'Go ahead,' he said.

Carefully Jan made other incisions with a scalpel, passed a probe through to the base of the puncture wound and then inserted rubber drains, using a pair of sinus forceps. All the time she was aware of her colleague's assessing watchfulness. With a pair of sharp-edged scissors she cut away the rotting tissue and skin that edged the main wound. The awful smell was now tempered somewhat by the odors of disinfectant and iodine.

When the three drains were in place to her satisfaction, Jan carefully stitched each one in place with some sterile black silk thread on a straight needle. 'That looks better,' she commented when she had finished.

'I can see you're a surgeon,' Gerard commented.

Jan shot him an acknowledging look, but said nothing. He had deliberately let her do the irrigation and debridement of the wound while he had watched her like a hawk. They would put on a loose padding and dressing, arranged so that it could be easily removed to allow for the frequent irrigation that would have to take place over the next few days.

'We'll keep him here for a few hours, do another irrigation ourselves and start him on intramuscular antibiotics as well as the I.V. stuff,' he said crisply from above her bent head, appearing to assume command. 'I want to monitor him myself for a while before we move him. He's probably feeling horribly nauseated from the infection, although he's not the sort of man to mention it. We'll give him some I.V. anti-nausea medication when he wakes up. That should cover the ride to the town.'

'How are we going to get him to Fort Roche?' Jan looked up, flexing her shoulders, stiff from bending over the patient's foot.

'I hope you'll agree to the use of your father's Land Rover,' he said. 'Would your father mind?'

'I shouldn't think so,' she said.

They looked at each other across the narrow width of the treatment table between them. For now he seemed to have accepted her, Jan sensed with an odd frisson of awareness. That acceptance was probably conditional on future performance.

How *she* felt about *him* was something she was reluctant to examine right now. Two doctors could not work together without some sort of attachment or antipathy developing fairly quickly. The work they did was very emotionally charged and co-operation very necessary.

The drive to Fort Roche in the early afternoon was considerably easier than her journey out of it had been the week before. Jan carefully steered her father's vehicle along the winding road into the outskirts of the town, avoiding other cars, minibuses, bicycles, pedestrians and the odd dog.

Gerard was squeezed in the back with Etienne, who was sprawled in a semi-sitting position along two-thirds of the

back seat, with his foot elevated, still stuporous from the
effects of the painkillers they had given him. Before leaving, they had seen several other patients at the clinic.

'The best way to get to the hospital is to go past the
docks—bypass the centre of the town, which is an absolute
zoo.' Gerard leaned forward over the back of her seat, gesturing the direction she should take. 'There's only one set
of traffic lights.'

They could see the old covered marketplace ahead of
them, where the buying and selling activities spilled out
into the street, fruit and vegetable sellers vying with each
other for customers. Inside there would be basket sellers,
bread and baked goods, meat, clothing and shoes, plus almost everything else that you could want on the island for
basic needs.

'Take that right turn before we get to the market.' His
head was close to hers as he directed her. She could smell
soap and iodine from his arms, and the scent of clean sweat.

As they passed the docks they saw a huge cruise ship,
towering like a palace above the water line. It looked incongruous among the utilitarian sheds and warehouses, a
touch of luxury quite out of place in the surrounding poverty that was hard to disguise. Jan gave it a quick glance,
her hair brushing against Gerard's face as she turned her
head. She wondered whether she should apologize and
stared ahead in confusion, with no words coming readily
to mind.

'While we're at the hospital we'll pick up the supplies
for the clinic,' Gerard said smoothly, filling the small, awkward void. 'They'll have some stuff waiting for us that was
ordered before the hurricane. No one's had time to pick it
up.'

The town of Fort Roche was built over a series of small
hills, the more affluent residential areas situated high up
among verdant vegetation where the cooling sea breezes

wafted lazily. Jan breathed deeply of the familiar scent of pungent soil, vegetation and ripe fruit, overlaid with a faint odor of drains and petrol fumes, as she negotiated the narrow streets. The hospital was some way up a hill, the streets *en route* bordered by low walls festooned with flowering plants, the colours brilliant in the sunshine.

'Take a left turn here,' Gerard instructed as they entered the forecourt of the hospital grounds. 'Go round to the casualty and admitting department. That's where they'll be waiting for us.'

The Royal Hospital, opened many years before by a minor member of the British royal family, was a small three-story building made of stucco-covered concrete. At first glance the whole place looked as though it could use a large injection of money. Various small extensions to the main building had been tacked on here and there.

It did not take long to hand over Etienne to the young house surgeon in charge of surgical admissions, explain the treatment they had given him and what they had planned for him.

'I'll call in to see him tomorrow,' Gerard said, after ascertaining to which of the surgical wards Etienne would be going. Their patient, still under the influence of drugs, opened his eyes long enough to smile weakly and wave in their direction as they took their leave.

'I'll telephone this evening to find out how he's doing,' Gerard said, striding along a corridor away from the casualty department. 'Now I'll show you where the bacteriology labs are. We'll leave these swabs for culture there, then we'll pick up our supplies from the pharmacy department.'

During the clean-up of Etienne's foot they had taken several swabs for the bacteriology lab. They would be cultured and would show them in a few days what bacteria were, or had been, growing in the infected foot.

As Jan hurried to keep up with Gerard she took a good look around, shocked by the lack of facilities that she saw and by the basic nature of the equipment. Although everything was clean, overlaid with the scent of disinfectant, there was a depressing run-down air about it all, a lack of basic maintenance. There were bare patches on the walls where paint had peeled off. Patients lay in old iron bedsteads on which the paint was also peeling.

'I'm glad to see they've got modern intravenous equipment,' she commented drily as they passed yet another ward.

'They have everything that's really necessary,' he said.

The pharmacist, a local man, greeted them warmly. 'How do you do? Welcome to St Bonar,' he said to Jan when introductions were made. 'We're extremely grateful that you have come to help us in our hour of need. God bless you!'

'I'm very glad to be here,' she said, meaning it with all her heart, touched by his words. It was very evident that this place needed all the help it could get.

'The supplies have been waiting for you for over a week, Dr Gerard,' the pharmacist said. 'If we hadn't been so busy here we might have delivered them for you. Maybe you'd like to check them.'

'Thanks a lot, Harry,' Gerard said.

Inside the pharmacy they went through the check list in an insulated metal case of supplies. 'This list was made up by Anne,' the pharmacist explained, leaving them to it.

There were sterile syringes, hypodermic needles, sterile cannulae and plastic giving-sets for intravenous fluids, rubber gloves, dressings of sterile gauze and antiseptics, among other things. There was another list of injectable drugs and oral drugs which were being kept cold.

Jan ran her eyes slowly down the list, gauging how she would have to use each item. Among the drugs listed were antibiotics, vials of local anesthetic, tetanus toxoid, as well as drugs for the more common general medical ailments. These supplies were simply to augment those already at the clinic, to keep them up to par, and obviously had to last for some time. Expertly, Gerard checked off each item as she called it out.

'We'll go out via the main entrance lobby,' Gerard said, carrying the heavy metal case effortlessly. 'That should just about complete your tour of the main part of the hospital. I'll show you the operating theatres some other time. It's just possible that you might be required to assist with an operation now and again, just to give someone else a much needed break—if that's all right with you?'

'I'd be quite happy to give someone else a break,' she said, more at ease now that they had deposited their patient safely.

In the lobby of the hospital, near the main double entrance doors, a small group of people stood, talking loudly. Some of the accents were American. Her colleague might have replied to her comment had her face not suddenly become suffused with shock.

'Oh, my God!' She whispered the words, albeit loud enough for him to hear, her eyes riveted on the group.

Dr Don McLean, whom she had not seen for some time, was just about recognizable to her, although he had put on weight and had become more bald since her last visit to the island. If nothing else, he would have been recognizable by his Scottish accent. It was one of the people with him who had caught Jan's startled attention as she came to an abrupt halt, her hand to her mouth.

'What is it? Do you know those people?' Gerard stopped beside her, frowning down at her.

'Yes...' she breathed. 'That's...that's Roderick Clairmont, the plastic surgeon from my hospital in Boston.'

'That's one of the names on the list of possible visiting

surgeons, I believe,' Gerard said. 'We get a lot of professional visitors here.'

'Hey, Gerard! Gerard!' Don McLean's ebullient voice broke over them. 'Come over here, man!'

The doctor came towards them with his arms outstretched, his short, rotund and paunchy body making him seem like an over-eager puppy. Behind his benign exterior was a sharp intelligence and shrewdness which had enabled him to keep the medical services on the island functioning against vast odds.

These thoughts flashed through Jan's mind as her upper arms were grasped. 'You must be Janine! I can't say I exactly recognize you. You were always a bonnie lass, and now you're as bonnie as they come! Isn't that right, Dr de Prescy?' He grinned at his colleague, deliberately using his surname to add credence to any observation about her beauty that he might declare.

Jan felt her features stiffen as she briefly looked over Don McLean's shoulder at Roderick Clairmont, John's father. How would he view her now? she wondered. Because she had dared to open her mouth, his son had transferred to another hospital.

Dragging her gaze back to Dr McLean's flushed face, she was dimly aware that he had paid her an exaggerated compliment and that something was perhaps expected of her. 'Um...' she began.

Gerard came to her rescue. 'As you say, Don,' he agreed, his voice husky, 'she's a bonny lass, but—' he lowered his voice '—I don't think she enjoys having it pointed out.' The rueful grin he gave his colleague belied any implied criticism.

Dr McLean was immediately contrite. He leaned forward to plant a quick kiss on Jan's cheek. 'Welcome to the team, Jan, even if it is for a short while. I apologize for not being at the clinic to greet you. I have this visiting group of surgeons from the States to show around the hospital and the whole island. We're thinking of setting up a small private hospital somewhere for them to operate in—plastic surgery, hernias, that sort of stuff.'

'Yes, I see,' Jan said, hoping that he would not take too much note of her glazed expression and stilted response. 'Dr de Prescy did...er...mention it.'

'The only snag is that we haven't got a site yet,' the doctor went on, seeming not to notice. 'These guys are some of the possible surgeons. Come over and meet them, Jan...Gerard.'

Grasping her arm, he led her forward. Dr Clairmont recognized her immediately. When he took her hand, giving it a firm squeeze, she knew that he was too mature a man to bear any sort of grudge. Also, he knew his own son.

'Well, this is quite a coincidence. Good to see you again, Jan.' That was all he said.

While Gerard stood, talking, Jan withdrew to the periphery of the group, then entered a ladies' cloakroom off the lobby. All the memories of her turmoil with John had come back and she found that her hands were shaking.

From her bag she took a hairbrush and raked it through her hair, stalling for time, before she tied it up again with the ribbon. In the mirror her wide, startled eyes stared back at her. Marvelling that she looked much calmer than she felt, Jan dabbed her flushed cheeks with a light powder, hoping that the group would have gone when she emerged. She and Gerard had to get back to the clinic, where Gerard had left his car.

'Would you like me to drive? We're going to be caught in the rush-hour traffic out of town. Maybe I can find some clear back streets,' Gerard offered as they at last emerged from the hospital to go to the Land Rover. Relieved not to

have seen Dr Clairmont again, yet still disturbed, Jan nodded assent and handed over the keys.

Driving on St Bonar required all one's concentration, especially in and around Fort Roche where the roads were
narrow, with many blind bends.

'It'll take us a while to get there,' Gerard commented
when they were on their way, 'with the roads being the
way they are. You'd be surprised how a few extra cars on
the road can clog things up.'

'Yes...' she agreed. Not usually at a loss for words, she
found herself oddly tongue-tied. If her companion felt any
curiosity about her and Dr Clairmont, he did not display it
openly. For that she was grateful. Obviously his manners
were good this time.

With her eyes closed, leaning back against the upholstery
which had become hot from the sun, she tried to relax as
the breeze from the window fanned her face. The presence
of Gerard de Prescy seemed to fill the whole vehicle and
she turned her head away from him towards the window.
They spoke little on the journey.

CHAPTER SIX

As THEY entered the village of Eden Bay Gerard did not turn the vehicle up the winding hillside road to the clinic, as Jan had expected, but drove along a road next to the beach, where the breakers rolled in onto a long crescent of white sand, shaded by coconut palms. A few brightly painted fishing boats had been hauled up onto the sand here and there. This was not a bathing beach for tourists but very much a working village, belonging to the local people.

When he pulled up beside the beach road, under the shade of a cluster of trees, Jan looked at him enquiringly.

'I don't know about you,' he said, stretching his arms wearily above his head, 'but I'm going for a quick swim. Coming?'

'Well... I haven't got a bathing suit with me,' she said, looking with longing at the blue water, sparkling in the sun.

'Neither have I,' he said, getting out. 'There's no one here at this time of the day—they're gutting the catch elsewhere. Even so, if you leave the vehicle, lock up.'

While she watched, he walked away from her to the edge of the water, where he quickly stripped down to his underwear, then splashed through the shallows to deeper water where he plunged in.

The sight was too much for Jan. She *had* brought a small towel with her which she had intended to use when she washed her hands at work. She hesitated for only a few moments, then locked the car and ran down on bare feet through the warm, fine, sand to the water's edge, carrying her sandals. There was no one else around to see her as she quickly divested herself of the cotton skirt and skimpy

blouse in the shelter of some scrubby bushes. Her underwear could, from a distance, easily pass for a bikini.

The water was heavenly, warm and very buoyant from
an excess of dissolved minerals. In moments Jan was float-
ing on her back, looking up at the sky. Late afternoon was
a lovely time of day when the intense heat was over and
the sky promised an early dusk. She closed her eyes and
allowed her body to be wafted by the tide, revelling in the
caress of the elements on her bare skin. The agitation she
had felt at the encounter with Dr Clairmont gradually began
to recede.

She came out before Gerard did. She towelled herself
down as best she could and dressed again, knowing that
her clothes would dry quickly.

'Could I borrow your towel?' Gerard said just behind her
as she bent to buckle her sandals.

'Yes.' Jan squinted up at him, being careful not to stare.
'It's rather damp.' Now that there was no specific work
issue to distract them, the atmosphere between them was
charged with a renewed tension. Jan hesitated to bring up
the issue of Manara, yet it wasn't far from her thoughts.

'Thanks.'

He had a superb physique, his muscles firm and smooth.
His wet hair was slicked back. Jan appraised him covertly,
as she had done during their hike through the woods. With
him now she felt a little like an actor who had forgotten
her lines and was trying to ad lib, except that she could
think of little to say. Anyway, she would be happy when
he left her to run the clinic her own way, even though he
would be there some of the time, she told herself.

'When we've checked back at the clinic,' he said, handing her back the towel, 'would you like to walk along the
beach to the fish market? I'll treat you to a flying-fish sandwich. The women do a bit of cooking there. After that walk
we might be ready for more cooling down in the water.'

'That would be great,' she agreed. 'I'm just realizing that I'm starving.' There had only been time earlier for a quick snack lunch.

There was no one waiting for them back at the clinic. Gerard tacked up a sign on a noticeboard by the door, informing the public that the clinic would be open the next day from ten o'clock.

'Do you think I'll be busy tomorrow?' Jan asked, when they were inside, doing some final clearing up from their earlier cases.

'Oh, sure. They'll come to get a look at you, if nothing else,' he said, smiling slightly as though at some private joke of his own. 'Some of them will suddenly find an urgent reason to see you about a medical condition that they've had for years, or a birth anomaly about which they intend to do nothing. All the time they'll be sizing you up. They're an interesting lot of people around here.'

'So I've noticed. Should one of us go in to see Etienne tomorrow?' she asked.

'Yes. I'll go. I live in Fort Roche, up in the hills overlooking the harbour. It's not far from the hospital,' he said. 'You can go in, if you want to, although it isn't necessary. Now, let me show you how the autoclave works so that we can sterilize the instruments we've used. As you've undoubtedly guessed, it's an old model. The nurse does all that stuff when she's here, of course.'

Later, when the clinic was once again securely locked up and they were about to get into their respective cars to leave for the fish market, Gerard reminded her again of his offer to buy their estate.

'Please tell your father that some visiting surgeons are on the island,' he said. 'They may want to have a look at Manara.'

The haughty look Jan gave him merely brought a slight raising of his eyebrows.

'It's far better, I think, to embrace change when the time's ripe—when it's inevitable—rather than to have that change thrust upon you by circumstances,' he remarked.

'Very convenient for you to say that. Is that some sort of threat?'

'No, of course not, Janine,' he said, his voice tinged with mild impatience. 'I'm merely pointing out what has been obvious to me for some time. He's ready to give up, whether he realizes it fully himself or not.'

'You mean that Roderick Clairmont will want to come to Manara?' she said, aghast. It had not occurred to her that they would invade her sanctuary.

'Possibly,' he said, 'as that is one of the proposed sites for a new clinic.'

Fueled by her discomfiture at meeting Dr Clairmont, she spoke sharply. 'Is it? I thought that was pure speculation at the moment. After all, we haven't sold it yet. Don't make the assumption that it's a *fait accompli*, Dr de Prescy.'

'Is he the one you had the unfinished business with?' he asked, lounging easily beside his car, one hand on top of the open door, as they stood beneath the calabash tree, with the golden rays of the evening sun playing over them.

'Unfinished…?'

'Was he your lover?'

'No! Of course not. It was his son.' Breathing rapidly, Jan looked at him with annoyance. How easily he had divined her dilemma and extracted the admission from her that John had been her lover.

He shrugged nonchalantly. 'Some women like older men,' he said.

Compressing her lips, Jan merely looked at him for a few moments. 'Shall we get to the fish market,' she said tartly, 'before they run out of fish?' It would not be a good idea to quarrel with him on her first day of work.

'You follow me,' he said, a knowing amusement in his voice. 'Don't run away, will you?'

'You're quite a mind-reader,' she said tartly. 'Since I have the faster car, I might just do that.'

'Ah, but I have the experience of the roads. I could catch you easily.'

The sky was streaked with red and orange from the setting sun as they drove back to the same spot on the beach where Gerard had parked before. From here they could walk along the beach to the fish market.

The flying-fish sandwiches, composed of breaded, delicately spiced fried fish in a type of pita bread, were delicious. They washed the food down with local beer, then ate slices of mango, before walking back along the beach for another dip in the sea. Dusk would be upon them very quickly. This was the best time of the day to be on the beach, in the more gentle, benign heat of the dying day.

The water was almost as still as a pond when they walked into it, with only a slight undertow which was never entirely absent. It was a pull that could lure you out to sea if you were not careful—could suck you out of your depth, bit by bit, where you could not cope unless you were a superb swimmer.

'Stay close to me.' Gerard was beside her in the water, which came up to her shoulders. 'This is high tide. The calm is deceptive.'

Jan did not bother to remind him that she knew all about the undertow. As the water wafted against them his skin came into contact with hers, tinglingly.

Jan shivered and drew back, the concept of being out of one's depth seeming uncannily apt with this man, a man whose quiet strength and willpower could stealthily sap your resistance. How frightened it made her feel that she should think of him as a tide, when here she was in that element with him... Abruptly she turned from facing out to sea so that she could focus on the safety of the shoreline in the fading light.

They swam and floated languidly in the warm, velvet-soft water until they could see the orange ball of the sun sink over the horizon. It left a cooler light behind it, reflected on the dark water. Touching bottom and feeling a few rocks underfoot, Jan began to swim and wade ashore, fighting against the pull of the undertow.

'Ouch,' she said softly, feeling a sharp sting in her left foot. She knew instantly what it was and trod water, not wanting to put weight on that foot.

'What is it?' Gerard was suddenly next to her, his face shadowy above the water, a dark silhouette.

'I think I've trodden on a sea urchin,' she said. 'It feels like it. Hell! What a nuisance.'

'Here, let me help.'

They came slowly out of the clinging surf, his arm around her and supporting her against his body so that she could hop. When they were out, he lifted her into his arms and carried her up onto the dry sand, lowering her onto it. 'Better deal with it right away. Stay there. I've got some stuff in my car.'

'Damn!' Jan swore to herself as Gerard disappeared into the shadows towards the parked car. There was no mistaking the sting of a sea urchin spine imbedded in a foot. The classic treatment was to drip hot candle wax onto the spine, not to try to pull it out as it invariably broke off, leaving part still in the foot. The spine would be clearly visible, like a black needle. The hot wax had the effect of sterilizing the wound and causing the spine to disintegrate. Otherwise, it could become infected.

Jan lay back on the sand while Gerard knelt beside her and raised her foot onto his knee to look at the sole with a flashlight. Very conscious of her skimpy underwear, plastered to her body with water, she tried to concentrate on the stinging sensation in her foot.

'I can see it there,' he said. In the glow of the flashlight she watched his frowning face. 'Roll over onto your stomach—that's the best position for me to drop the wax onto the foot. You're going to have to be brave for a few seconds...you won't feel the heat for more than that.'

'Thank you,' Jan said, and turned over, feeling the warm sand sticking to her bare, moist skin. 'I feel like an idiot for not being more careful about the rocks. Sorry to be such a nuisance.' The sea urchins generally clung to rocks that were away from the pounding surf. She should have remembered.

'Can't be helped,' he murmured.

Jan cradled her head on her bent arms and waited while he lit the candle after several attempts, cupping the flame with his hands against the breeze.

'OK, Jan,' he said softly, his voice husky with an unaccustomed tenderness which, she had noted, he sometimes used with his patients. Maybe this would be the only time he would be really in sympathy with her, she thought wryly, although several times today he had used the diminutive of her name...without being invited to do so. 'Take a deep breath, here comes the wax. Try not to jerk away or I'll just have to do it again.'

'Ouch... Oh!' Closing her eyes and gritting her teeth, Jan waited for the worst of the pain to pass. After a few seconds the searing heat faded. With it, over the next few moments, went the stinging pain that had preceded it.

'It really does work. That's wonderful! Can I sit up now?' In the light from the candle and the small flashlight her near nakedness was very evident. 'Could you switch off that flashlight, please? We are sort of spotlighted here. I would rather not have an audience while I'm like this.' She laughed nervously.

'Just a moment. I want to put some iodine around the puncture area. Don't put the foot down on the sand—keep it clean.'

'Maybe I'll be able to return the service some time,' she quipped, feeling vulnerable and shy with him as she lay flat on her stomach with one foot in the air, clad in transparent underwear.

'Maybe you will,' he said, laughter in his voice, 'but I'm not going to step on a sea urchin just so that you can return the compliment of dropping hot wax on my foot. I could think of more pleasant ways of...being ministered unto by you. Preferably not of a professional nature...'

When he laughed it was an open, genuinely amused laugh, not suggestive or insinuating as it might have been with many men. Jan sensed that it was not his way to insinuate—he would ask outright if he wanted something.

'Do you usually carry a candle and matches with you for this purpose?' she blurted out, hyper-aware now of his closeness, his stillness, as he knelt beside her, waiting for the iodine to dry on her foot so that he could apply a strip of plaster. Obligingly, he clicked off the flashlight.

Peering sideways from her prone position, Jan looked at his brooding, dark face, mysterious in the feeble, wavering light of the candle. There was a tightness in her chest, an anticipation, as he returned her gaze.

'Sure,' he said softly. 'They're part of the standard first-aid kit here. As a child of the islands, you should know that.'

'I...suppose I did know it at one time. I knew what to do, of course.'

'How does the foot feel now?'

'Um...more or less normal, just a bit odd.' She tried to make light of it, conscious of his hand still touching her foot. 'Thank you. I'm very grateful...Gerard.'

'My pleasure,' he said. 'You can sit up now. Careful...'

When she struggled to a sitting position she saw and felt that her whole body was covered with sand. One of her bra straps had fallen down over her shoulder onto her upper arm, dragging down the material freeing her breast from its covering. As she moved a hand to cover herself Gerard's hand came up over hers, stilling her movement.

'Don't,' he said quietly.

Swiftly she looked up at him to see an unmistakable message on his face, his eyes intent with a fierce desire. With his eyes still on hers and his face close, he leaned forward and blew out the candle that he held between them.

Momentarily blinded, Jan could just make out the dark shape of his head, coming closer to hers, then felt his lips touch her mouth. A small animal sound of shock and—she recognized it— sexual longing came involuntarily from her throat as sharp desire flooded her with an enveloping warmth. The effect was powerful, paralyzing, as his mouth covered hers.

The hand that touched her breast caressed her gently and moved over her, exploring, pushing aside the damp material which was gritty with sand. An incoherent sound of protest came from her as she jerked her mouth away from his, the fingers on her breasts feeling like trails of fire. She found her voice and whispered, 'No...no.'

With uncertain, fumbling movements she pushed at him ineffectually, trying to distance herself from him. I mustn't get involved with him. The frantic thought pounded in her brain.

'Jan...Jan...' He murmured her name and she was aware that he was trembling and that his breathing was harsh and uneven. To many men, sex was a calculated thing, something to be exploited—she had found that out in the last few years. Gerard de Prescy, strong, in command, competent, wanted her—trembled with his need of her. And she needed him. She could not lie to herself.

If only he had not had to touch her, this would not have happened. It rekindled thoughts of that earlier swift and unexpected contact. An old saying of the islands came to her, of desire between former lovers, 'It don't take much kindling for the old fire stick to ketch back up.'

Through her half-closed eyes, as her head was thrown back, she saw his dark shape against the evening sky, where pale indigo met streaks of pink and orange. In moments they would be in total darkness. With her hands still on his shoulders, holding him away from her, she struggled against the tightness in her chest, the momentary panic before surrender.

'Jan...' Again he whispered her name, waiting tensely for her to acquiesce. Instinctively, she knew that he would never force her into anything. A swift intuition told her that he had not desired a woman in this way for a long time and that he was, above all, a man who would choose his women carefully—at least, those women he would be serious about.

With a sudden convulsive movement she let go of him so that he could pull her against him and crush her soft breasts against his hard, powerful body. With a groan of pleasure that was a recognition of their mutual desire, he kissed her with a fierce hunger, moving his mouth exploringly over hers. In moments she was responding mindlessly, straining him to her, where seconds before she had repelled him.

He eased her down so that they lay side by side on the sand. Their bodies strained together, his hand tangling in her damp hair. For a long time they kissed, his mouth demanding a response that she was more and more willing to give. Her trembling hands stroked the skin of his back. There was a soft soughing of the breeze in the coconut palms nearby, the swish of surf.

We don't know each other... We don't know each

other... Somewhere, from a distance, that warning came to her as she felt his hand smooth down her back, over her hips, her thighs. In that touch there was a rare protectiveness, a gentleness...beyond words...as well as need. The sound of the surf became muted and all she was aware of was the uneven tenor of his breathing, superimposed on her own, and the beating of their hearts.

As they lay side by side on the sand he gathered her closely to him. Unresistingly, she let her pliant body stay in the circle of his arms, and a rare joy and a kind of peace came over her, mingling with a sharp, mindless desire.

A rare car, going along the coast road, broke into their trance-like state, its headlamps momentarily lighting their sanctuary. It turned down onto a small parking area beside the beach, not far from where they had parked their cars. The sound of music from a radio came to them.

'We...we had better go,' Jan whispered.

'Mmm...' Gerard murmured, kissing her closed eyelids. 'Scared I might lose control, Jan?' There was teasing laughter in his voice as he eased back from her and ran a hand tantalizingly over her abdomen.

'I...wouldn't flatter myself,' she whispered back, as her heard pounded a response.

He laughed softly, deep in his throat. 'You *can* flatter yourself...if you want to.' He said the words against her ear, his warm breath like a caress.

Jan smiled, knowing that he could feel the small movement of her smile when he put his cheek against hers.

'Do you want to?' he said.

There were voices nearby and louder music, as though someone was preparing to have a small beach party.

'Mmm?' he persisted.

'I'll have to think about that.' Suddenly she wanted to laugh deliriously.

'So you're a tease,' he said, smiling.

'No...I think actions speak for themselves.'

With that, he kissed her mouth, her shoulders, her breasts...

'We'd better go. Hmm?' he said at last, his voice thick with frustrated need. 'Before we find ourselves in the middle of a party.'

'Yes...'

'Put this on.' He helped her into his long-sleeved shirt, having gathered their clothes when he'd gone for the first-aid kit.

It was a while before they reluctantly moved. 'I'll carry you to the car,' he said, not giving her a choice. 'Put your shoes on right away. Here, you carry our clothes. Do you think you can manage to drive?'

'I think so.'

'You drive in front of me then, if you run into trouble, I'll be right there behind you.'

That night Jan lay sleeplessly in bed, staring at the ceiling. This time the tree frogs kept her company—she almost welcomed their infernal noise. Earlier she had thought of John Clairmont, and her feelings for him. It seemed that she had been in love with the idea of him, rather than the reality...an immature love.

She had remembered his bitter accusations that she had deliberately tried to ruin his career, by making him look incompetent. Nothing had been further from the truth—she had been thinking of the patient's life. His vindictiveness had been shocking.

Bewildered and hurt at the time, she had retreated from him—and from any deep involvement with other men. Indeed, she had welcomed those who had clearly wanted nothing more than a superficial emotional relationship, with or without a sexual component.

The image of another man, dark and compelling, as though waiting in the wings, came to dominate her mind.

A ceiling fan moved the warm air languidly, inadequately, above her as her whole body seemed to burn with frustration, her mind coming to focus on nothing else but Gerard de Prescy. Thoughts of him seemed to fill her whole being, as though he were actually there.

In a few weeks she would be leaving here, and they would get on with their separate lives. One part of her was appalled that they had lain together semi-naked on her very first day of working with him. Another part of her knew, with an uncanny certainty, that if the circumstances were right they would come together in an explosive sexual union that would have had no parallel with her.

Perhaps she had better take steps to ensure that the circumstances were never right...

CHAPTER SEVEN

EARLY morning sunlight tinted the tops of trees from low on the horizon the next day when Jan and her father sat on the front verandah, drinking mango juice and eating the toast she had made for breakfast. Her father ate little, first taking an antacid tablet from a bottle on the table.

The towering, majestic cabbage palms, which stood like sentries along the driveway, rustled their branches in the sea breeze. This was the perfect time to admire the beauty of the place.

There was a faint smell of smoke from the smoke-house, the place where the coconut kernels were dried for copra. It was an indication that at least some of her father's staff, such as they were, had returned to work. Sometimes he could not afford to pay those workers so he let them grow their crops on his land free in lieu of wages. It was an arrangement that seemed to work. The manager, on the other hand, was always paid.

Jan knew that she presented a calm, cool exterior, dressed in slim white trousers and a pale yellow cotton shirt, with her hair pulled back neatly from her face, yet inside her emotions were churning. Wanting to see Gerard again, she hoped, perversely, that he would not be at the clinic for a few days so that she would have a chance to regain her composure.

'Keep that appointment in mind, Dad, that I told you about last night,' she said, pouring herself coffee. 'For the gastroscopy, with Dr McLean. I'll drive you in to Fort Roche myself and stay with you while they do it. Normally it's a day procedure, but Dr McLean said he'll probably keep you in the hospital overnight just to keep an eye on you as we *are* quite a long way from town.'

'Oh, yes. Tell me again what's involved with that.' It was typical that he sounded a little vague, a little surprised that she was taking his condition very seriously, even though he had called her to come. Feeling reasonably well again, he wanted to pretend that he was quite all right. Perhaps he had thought that he could relax now that she was here, forgetting that she would have to leave again.

'They'll look into your stomach with a long scope,' she explained. 'It's a flexible tube with a light at the end, which goes down your throat. You won't feel a thing—you'll be sedated. Dr McLean can have a good look around inside.'

'Sounds all right,' he said.

Jan sighed, sipping her coffee. The sooner that diagnostic procedure was done the better.

Her father's increasing exhaustion seemed to stare her in the face every time she looked at him. It was becoming increasingly clear that he would have to spend less time on St Bonar and more in England. They could let the tourist board take over, allow them to let it out to paying guests— that was always an option if they could renovate a little. They would need money for that.

'Hilda's coming back today,' her father said, 'and the phones are working. I noticed that this morning.'

'Great!' Jan smiled. 'Things are looking up. I'll be able to phone you from the clinic, keep tabs on you.'

Hilda was the sixteen-year-old-daughter of Theresa, the housekeeper, who had taken care of Manara for many years. Hilda had a room at Manara for the occasional times that she was there. Mostly she was still in school, only coming to help her mother out. Theresa herself was away, having gone back to Eden Bay before the hurricane to be with her other children. Now Hilda had come to do the cooking.

'I thought I'd phone Mum today,' Jan said. 'She needs to know what's happening.'

'Yes, I'll phone her too,' her father said quickly, 'but I don't want her dashing out here until she has to.'

'Have you assessed the storm damage yet, Dad?' Jan ventured as she sipped her tea, changing the subject. She would make sure that her mother knew the gist of what was really going on.

'Just about,' he sighed. 'Things don't look good.'

'There were some visiting doctors at the hospital yesterday. Gerard de Prescy said to tell you that they might want to look at Manara.' She passed on the news reluctantly.

'Oh, really?' Her dad perked up, his tired face looking hopeful. 'You don't like him much, do you, Jan?'

'Well...'

'I think you're mistaken there. He's a good man.'

'Then you do want to sell, Dad?'

'I don't want to,' he conceded. 'I'm coming round to the idea that it may be inevitable. It's not every day that you get an offer in a place like this. Some properties are on the market for years. It may be either that or the tourist board.'

'I know you can't run a business on nostalgia,' she said sadly. They had teamed up with other plantation owners years ago to form the Federation of Banana Growers to help spread their losses. There was little else they could do. Even with the hurricane damage, they could possibly still pull through by dint of hard work, if only her father had a will to do so. 'Perhaps I can think of something, find another way.'

'There is nothing else,' Jack Newsome seemed almost in tears. 'Don't think I haven't thought about it ad nauseam.'

A clock in the adjacent sitting room chimed seven. In another fifteen minutes Jan would leave for work. This was the best time of the day in which to get things done, before the heat that came at around ten o'clock. 'Are you sure you don't need the car, Dad?' she asked him yet again.

'No, you take it.'

'There's dengue in Trinidad,' Jan said, remembering what Gerard had told her.

'Hell!' Jack Newsome said. 'Make sure you take precautions. Better sleep under the mosquito netting from tonight. That's all we need!'

'I'll see you later, then. I'll phone. Take care.'

There were no other cars parked under the calabash tree when she arrived at the clinic. In a few minutes she had unlocked the door, opened windows and turned on the ceiling fans.

She had brought with her a huge book on internal medicine. In the lull of early morning she took the opportunity to look up dengue fever, which was not something one generally encountered. While her ears strained for the sound of a car, she leafed through the heavy tome.

'There is no drug to cure dengue', she read, 'and no vaccine to prevent it. In areas where the fever is endemic it is important that householders get rid of any containers that could hold stagnant water or collect water after rain, where the *Aëdes aegypti* mosquito could breed'.

Among the symptoms, she read, was an abrupt onset of a high fever, together with a severe frontal headache and pain behind the eyes, as well as the muscle and joint pains. Paracetamol was used, rather than aspirin, to control the fever.

That species of mosquito existed on St Bonar, she knew, even though vigorous efforts were made constantly to get rid of the breeding grounds. Don McLean never let anyone forget it. The main sources of infection were people coming in from other islands, who were then bitten by the local mosquito.

The telephone on the desk in front of her rang at that moment, making her jump.

'Good morning, Jan.' The voice of the man she was hoping to avoid for a while broke through her spurious composure.

'Um…good morning.' She forced a calmness. 'Are you coming here today? Or am I going to be alone?'

'I won't be there today,' he said, as though he could sense her tension. 'Maybe not tomorrow either. I have some operating to do at the Royal Hospital. Anne, the nurse, will get there as soon as she can. You can always phone me here if you need to. I'll give you the number.'

Jan had been holding her breath. Now she let it out on an audible sigh. Quickly she scribbled down the number he gave her—of the surgeons' lounge in the operating theatres.

'Relieved?' he said softly, laughing at her.

'N—' She was about to deny it. 'Yes, if you want the truth.'

'The truth is always best, Jan. I'm looking forward to seeing you again.'

It was fortunate that he couldn't see her as her cheeks suffused with betraying colour.

'How's your father?' he queried.

'No worse.'

'I've spoken to Don McLean this morning about the gastroscopy. I'll see you then, if not before. That will be the first step.' There seemed to be a double meaning to his words, or maybe it was her over-active imagination, Jan chided herself.

'Yes. Well, goodbye, Dr de Prescy. I'll certainly call you if there's something I can't cope with.' Quickly she replaced the receiver.

Yesterday he had told their patient, Etienne, that he had been married once. Thinking about it now, she assumed that he was divorced. What an idiot she had been to get involved with him as much as she had done. Although she was relieved that he wasn't there, at the same time she was going to miss his presence at the clinic in an odd sort of way…and she was still angry.

Anne did not arrive that day or the next. On her own for two days, the hours seemed to fly by as she was forced to learn the routine of the job without delay. As Dr Jan Newsome she become something of a local celebrity overnight. Uncharacteristically, people turned up at the clinic with very minor aches and pains that they would not normally, she felt sure, have bothered to complain about—just to get a look at her, as Gerard had predicted.

The work certainly took her mind off other things. She would not have been surprised to learn, at the end of the two days, that the entire adult population of Eden Bay had made its way through the door of the clinic since she had arrived there, with more from the surrounding area besides. There had been plenty of children too.

In spite of the huge volume of work that the influx had given her, it had been a gratifying experience which had left her absorbed and surprisingly happy. The local people had a way of drawing others into the intricacies of their lives as they strove to make an adequate living.

It had become apparent to Jan during this time that usually, because resources were limited, the local population of St Bonar accepted illness with a certain stoic resignation. They probably only went to a doctor when they could no longer ignore the knowledge that they were ill—unless there was a new doctor to size up. She had seen old injuries, and the effects of diseases, which should have been attended to long ago.

Friday came soon enough, after a very busy week, the day scheduled for Jack's gastroscopy at the Royal Hospital in

Fort Roche. Dr McLean had arranged for the nurse to work at the Eden Bay clinic for the day.

They were both nervous when the day dawned, wondering what would be found. Jan got up early, and dressed in a cool cotton skirt and a sleeveless top. As she brushed her hair in front of the mirror in her bedroom, securing it away from her face in a knot on top of her head, she could not keep her thoughts away from the possibility that her father might have stomach cancer…or from the knowledge that Gerard had said he would see them at the hospital. She had not seen him since Monday, and his absence disturbed her for reasons that she could not explain.

It was laughable, really—she smiled mockingly at her reflection as she applied a pale lipstick that enhanced her honey-colored tan—that she should be sort of looking forward to seeing a man whom she had decided she ought to avoid, confused by the thought that he might be avoiding her. Such was life.

In the kitchen she got breakfast for herself. 'You haven't eaten anything, have you, Dad?' she queried when her father came into the kitchen, all ready for departure.

'No, I haven't,' he confirmed, 'and I'm starving. Nothing to eat or drink after midnight.'

'Good,' she said. His stomach had to be empty for this examination. Although he would not have a general anaesthetic, he would be heavily sedated.

'How long do you think the actual test will take?' he asked, forgetting that he had asked that question several times before. Jan knew only too well that people were so anxious when they had to undergo an operation or a test such as this one that they did not really hear answers and explanations that were given to them. That was why it was so important to explain things carefully, repeatedly, in terms that a lay person could understand, without talking down to them.

'The actual procedure will take about three quarters of an hour,' Jan explained, resisting the urge to put her arms round her father to comfort him, knowing that he was striving to maintain a certain dignity. 'Then for about an hour you'll sleep off the sedation. I expect Don McLean will talk to both of us later about what he found once you're wide awake.'

'Why do they want me to stay overnight? I could come home.'

They had been over all this before. 'Because we're a long way from town, Dad. It's just to make sure that there's no bleeding afterwards from your stomach. He's going to take a tiny biopsy, a little piece of the stomach lining, to send to the lab. There's a remote possibility that you might get some oozing from the biopsy site. It's just to be sure, that's all.' It was this biopsy which would determine whether he had cancer. That was something she did not want to tell him.

'Yes...' Jack nodded absently. 'Who would have thought it would come to this?'

'It hasn't really come to anything yet, Dad,' Jan said as she poured herself a glass of cool guava juice from the refrigerator, trying to inject cheerfulness into her voice. 'All you're having is a diagnostic test. After that we'll be in a better position to assess the situation. What happens with your health will definitely influence what we do with Manara.'

'Yes...' he said again, staring out of the window at the early morning sun. 'I have the feeling that it's time for change...whether we want it or not.'

Jan silently agreed with him, albeit reluctantly, as she spread two pieces of toast with a thin layer of home-made mango jam. A time of reckoning definitely seemed to be at hand. Her own life was in a state of flux too. When she had spent six months in her new job in the United States she might well return to England.

As it was, she'd only seen her mother and brother, who was at university, half a dozen times a year for the past four years, although they usually spent two or three weeks together at a time. All the travelling was expensive, even though she liked the global village idea. It was an odd, schizophrenic feeling sometimes, to have close ties to three places. Perhaps something had to give.

As though echoing her thoughts, her father mused quietly, 'It's not possible to do more than one thing really well at a time, so I've found, otherwise we become dabblers, voyeurs, dilettantes. The tragedy of human existence is that we can only live one life. Most of us try to live several when we really have only enough time and energy for one—especially time.'

'Yes,' Jan said.

'You know, you see people going from one marriage to the next, for instance, as though it will always be better the next time—as though they have a right to expect someone else to make them happy. So often it doesn't work. You have to make yourself happy.'

'You've never talked liked this before, Dad,' Jan said, considering his words. 'You must be getting philosophical in your old age.'

'I guess I am.' He smiled a little self-consciously.

'Sometimes you wonder what it's all about—what *you're* all about.'

Desperately wanting to comfort him yet not able to think of anything to say that would not sound trite at that moment, Jan carried the used crockery to the sink. Her throat felt tight with suppressed emotion.

'Shall I drive, Dad?' she said, gathering up her bag and small umbrella. There was a forecast of heavy, intermittent rain, which meant that there could well be a torrential downpour, like the monsoon, for about three to five minutes at a time. Usually it stopped suddenly, as though a tap had been turned off, leaving everything steaming in the hot sun.

'You'd better. I might pass out from lack of sustenance.'

Soon they were bouncing and lurching in the Land Rover over the temporary bypass road around the landslide, where they saw men and machines shifting earth, to get to the paved Fort Roche Road. The air was alive with the chirping of birds.

The room where the gastroscopies were done was on the second floor of the three-story hospital, next to a small day surgery post-operative and pre-operative unit. Don McLean was there to meet them. While her father was going through the brief admission procedures, Dr McLean spoke to Jan about him.

'If you would like to come in to look at the video screen once I've got the scope into his stomach,' he said, 'I'll send the nurse out to get you. Just wait in the corridor outside. Fortunately, for this procedure we've got all the latest equipment, which was donated to us.'

'Yes, I would like to see what you find,' Jan said, knowing he was fully aware of her apprehension. 'Thank you for getting him looked at so soon.'

'Well, Jan, if I'd known about this sooner I would have got him in months ago, believe me. He's a secretive man.'

'You're absolutely right.'

'You've been giving him the antibiotic, clarithromycin?' he asked. He was looking very businesslike, dressed in a green scrub suit and operating cap.

'Yes, the three drugs—clarithromycin, flagyl and the hydrochloric acid blocker,' Jan confirmed.

'That's great,' he said. 'Your dad's the first one on the list so we'll be getting him in soon. You go and get yourself a cup of coffee in the cafeteria on the ground floor, my girl.

Be back here in about half an hour and I should have something to show you.'

The kind words brought a pricking of tears to Jan's eyes and she blinked rapidly. 'Thank you.' The words came out in a whisper. 'I'll do that. I…I guess it's good for us doctors to be on the other side of the fence once in a while.'

'You bet!'

There were people waiting everywhere—in the corridors, in the entrance lobby—when she went to find the cafeteria. They were either patients or relatives waiting for patients, like herself. When she was seated at a small table by herself with a cup of watery coffee, which she did not really want, in front of her, Jan let her mind dwell fully on what the problem might be with her father.

It was not really fair to expect her father to hang on here in St Bonar to keep the failing estate going when it was clearly making him sick because of the stress.

'Hello, Jan.' A voice spoke directly above her head, jerking her out of her reverie. 'Don said you would be here. I've just been talking to your father.'

Gerard was there, lowering himself to the seat opposite. He, too, was wearing a scrub suit and looked tired. Jan felt herself stiffen away from him as her heart rate increased, in spite of her underlying, sobering anxiety. Would he show any evidence that he regretted his loss of control with her?

'Oh, hello.' She managed a small smile as she met his assessing glance. 'It's…um…it's nice to see someone else I know. Thanks for coming. I do appreciate it.'

There was no need to worry. As his dark eyes searched her pale, strained face she discerned a warmth in their depths. For the most part, he looked as though he had been working day and night since Monday. 'Sorry I couldn't get to the clinic over the past days. Things here have been crazy. We're still getting injuries from the storm…all sorts of stuff.'

'I understand,' she said quietly, staring into the muddy-looking liquid in her cup. 'How is Etienne? Is he still in the hospital? I was thinking that I'd like to see him while I'm here.'

'Yes, he's still here. The foot's much better.' Gerard smiled. 'Still a little pungent at times, but a different type of pungent.'

'I'm glad.'

'How are you? You're probably as worried as hell.'

'Yes, even though I suspect Dad's just got an ulcer. He has lost weight...'

'Don't forget that you haven't seen him for a while,' he said.

'Mmm...'

The hand he placed over hers for a moment as it rested on the table was warm and strong, a brief comforting gesture. 'We'll know soon enough. Try not to worry. I have to be in the operating theatres in about ten minutes. You know, you shouldn't be alone at Manara. I'd like to lend you one of my dogs for a night or two until you have more staff at the place.'

'That's...that's very kind of you,' she said.

'I've got two dogs. They're mastiffs, friendly to people they like, great guard dogs.'

'Maybe they won't like me.' She smiled. 'I haven't had much experience with dogs in the last little while.'

'I'll give you Pansy. She'll like you if I tell her to.' He grinned, and it transformed his tired face, showing his even, white teeth that contrasted with his tanned skin.

Steeling herself against his attraction, Jan nodded. 'All right. I shall enjoy having her. Thank you.'

He got up to leave. 'I'll be finished here after lunch. I'll meet you. Then I'll fetch the dog and drive back with you.'

Again she nodded, feeling a heavy, prophetic sense of inevitability. They would be alone at Manara...

Heads turned as he strode out of the room. People turned to look at her with a benign curiosity. No doubt they all knew Dr Gerard.

What had brought him to this place, this backwater? she wondered again. It was evident that he was a world-class doctor. On the other hand, he was just the sort of professional person that a place like St Bonar needed so desperately.

Forcing herself to sip the unappealing coffee, Jan saw from a wall clock that she had another twenty minutes to wait. The imprint of Gerard's fingers was still on her hand, a tingling sensation, oddly intimate.

The gastroscopy room was almost dark, the lights turned off, when she went in. There was a glow from the video screen as the fiber-optic scope that was in her father's stomach, via his esophagus, relayed pictures in brilliant colour to it. The nurse had come out to get Jan. Don McLean had an assistant, as well as the nurse, helping him.

'You can see there, Jan,' Dr McLean said in a low voice, pointing to the screen, 'that there are two ulcerated areas, side by side. Although each one is relatively small, as ulcers go, I wouldn't want to have those myself.'

The ruched lining of the stomach showed up red on the screen, with the two ulcerated areas, near the bottom end of the stomach, showing up a deeper, raw red. 'Yes,' Jan agreed, moving closer to the screen. 'It...it doesn't look like cancer to me. It looks like a regular ulcer. Is that what you think?'

'Yes, I do. We're going to take a few little biopsies from the margins of each ulcer, just to be on the safe side. There's evidence of healing already—the antibiotics you've been giving him have had a definite beneficial effect. Otherwise, I would have expected the ulcers to be much more raw-looking than they are.'

'That's a relief,' Jan said, meaning it with all her heart. Seeing her father there helpless on the operating table, sedated, with the end of the black flexible scope protruding from his mouth, she knew then that she had, like most offspring, taken her father for granted. Now, it seemed, she saw him in another way, with great clarity, for the first time.

She moved away from the screen that showed every detail of the interior of her father's stomach in almost lurid colour—the gastric juices, which were being sucked out slowly with the suction attached to the scope, the peristaltic movements of the muscles. Medical technology was enabling the human eye to see a part of a living person with a light and a special camera system that was normally only accessible during a surgical operation.

'We'll continue the drug treatment that he's getting now,' Don McLean was saying. 'We'll watch him carefully to make sure there's no perforation. The lining of the stomach's pretty thin in the ulcerated area, by the looks of it. I don't like the fact that he's got the two ulcers side by side like that. He should have come to me earlier...much earlier.'

As Jan quietly left the room, while Dr McLean prepared to take biopsies with a tiny punch-biopsy forceps, his words remained in her mind. They were not out of the woods yet. On the positive side, it was unlikely that her father had cancer, as a cancerous ulcerated area had a characteristic appearance to the naked eye, which was not present here. On that score, at least, she felt happy.

While her father recovered in the post-op area Jan went outside to walk in the gardens of the hospital. She enjoyed the feel of the sun on her bare skin, and started to relax. The muted sounds of the main part of the town in the near distance eddied around her. Coconut palms offered intermittent shade as she walked.

'You want grapefruit, missy? Mango?' A fruit seller,

who had set up a stall on the pavement on the other side of the wrought-iron fence that enclosed the hospital gardens, called to Jan, flashing her a winning smile.

Wanting to pass time as pleasantly as she could in the circumstances, and enjoy a day of freedom in the beautiful sunshine, Jan sauntered over to look at the woman's wares. Eventually she bought a bag of fruit of various types, as well as some vegetables.

CHAPTER EIGHT

THEY met when it was all over.

With her father sleeping peacefully in the small overnight ward, Jan had gone to see a rather bashful Etienne, who looked clean and decidedly healthier, before going to the lobby to meet Gerard.

He towered above the other people milling around in the reception area, as her eyes searched him out. With a slight smile of recognition he came towards her. Again a powerful sense of inevitability came over Jan as he seemed to claim her. What am I doing? she asked herself. There was, it seemed, no answer, other than the obvious one of instinct.

'I was beginning to think you hadn't waited for me.' He smiled, taking her arm to guide her through the throng, while Jan felt her throat tighten up so that she could not speak.

The drive to his house to pick up the dog passed by for her in a daze as she sat as a passenger in his car. The dog proved to be a large, beautiful, smoky-gray animal, with yellow eyes and a puppy-like clumsiness that was endearing. They drove back to the hospital to pick up her car.

As she drove the Land Rover back to Manara, the warm wind blowing in her hair from the open window, it was impossible not to be reminded of the first journey she had made in the eight-seater minibus not so long ago and of the man galloping after her on horseback. So much had happened since then that it seemed like months ago rather than two weeks. Also, life on the island was beginning to cast its spell over her.

Checking the rear-view mirror, she saw Gerard's battered

Ford saloon following her. In the back seat of his car was Pansy. Jan found herself grinning as she briefly saw the outline of the dog, swaying slightly with the motion of the car, and wondered how Gerard had arrived at that name.

As they turned off the temporary bypass road and onto the lane that went to Manara Jan noticed the increasing cloud in the sky. Bracing herself for the bumps ahead, she increased speed as much as she could to get to Manara before the predicted rain.

The rain came suddenly when they were in view of the house. A solid sheet of water—as though a giant in the sky had turned on a tap—immediately obscured the view of the track, and there was only a vague shimmering outline of the house up ahead. Rain drummed a deafening tattoo on the roof of the car as Jan inched the vehicle forward. The track would soon turn into a torrent of raging water and mud, she knew from experience.

Jan was forced to stop the car before she got to the house as the wheels began to skid in the mud. In the few seconds that it took her to get out and slam the door she was soaked to the skin, her thin trousers and yellow shirt plastered to her body, her breasts outlined as though she were naked. Being soaked to the skin when in the presence of Gerard de Prescy seemed to be her habitual *modus operandi* these days, she laughed to herself as her feet sank in the soft mud.

'Hey, take my hand,' Gerard shouted, and extended a hand to her, holding the dog's leash with the other, having stopped his car behind hers. His hair was flattened by water, his clothing in the same condition as her own, as they were pounded by rain that was warm, like a hot shower.

'I love the rain.' He was laughing, a sound that was infectious so that Jan found an absurd desire welling up in her, as she clasped his hand for much needed support, to give way to delirious mirth after the recent tension.

Carefully they picked their way through rushing mini-rivers, slipping and slithering through mud to the house, the dog keeping up with them stoically. At the steps to the house Gerard lifted his arms and face to the sky, letting the water splash into his mouth and over his closed eyelids. There was a strange exultation in him that communicated itself to Jan, a wild excitement as though he derived a pure, sensual pleasure from the experience.

'That's very hedonistic,' she commented, enjoying it herself, completely soaked.

'Yes…' he said jubilantly.

She ran up the steps ahead of him. Under the verandah the rain beat on the tin roof like the beating of a thousand drums.

Jan eased her feet out of her muddy sandals by the door. 'Come inside,' she called, watching him remove his shoes. Through the thin material of his soaked shirt she could see dark hairs, wet and flattened, on his chest and the outline of his powerful thighs under the covering of his linen trousers which were equally sopping.

A tremor of sexual awareness, that same sense of knowing that something must surely happen between them, gripped her with a fearful, clamorous certainty. It combined with the heady relief that she had felt at the hospital earlier to form a potent mix.

The deep, sonorous barking of Pansy added to the din of pounding water as she unlocked the door with clumsy hands.

In the hallway the dog went wild with excited curiosity on being in a new place. Having shaken herself, she gambolled around her master, waiting to be given permission to explore.

'Do you mind having a thoroughly wet dog exploring your house?' Gerard asked, going down on one knee to make a fuss of the dog. 'She has to get to know the territory she's defending.'

'No...no...I don't mind,' Jan said breathlessly, feeling as though she could not get enough air. Every part of his powerful body was outlined by his clinging, drenched clothing.

He turned and saw her looking at him unguardedly, and his expression changed. At once there was a charged tension. His eyes moved over her hotly—over her exposed, wet breasts with their taut nipples, over her thighs. 'Go... Go,' he said to the dog, gesturing with his arm.

Obediently Pansy trotted off in the direction of the kitchen at the back of the house, the nails on her substantial paws clicking rhythmically on the wooden floor as she went.

Very slowly Gerard stood up and reached out a hand for Jan. Unresistingly, she took it—she could not help herself. He led her into the sitting room and shut the heavy door behind them. The room was dim, the interior shutters closed. They stood looking at each other as he held both her hands captive.

Jan's chest rose and fell rapidly in anticipation. She felt again that she could scarcely get her breath, that she was mesmerized, as his eyes moved over her body as though he were stripping her naked.

I ought not to be here with him, like this, she told herself. But she wanted him, had allowed it to happen. She wanted him as she had never wanted a man before, as she had never imagined it would be possible to want someone...

'I think we have some unfinished business, don't you?' Gerard said, his voice low, his dark eyes seeming to burn into hers. There was a new light of a strange intentness in them, as though he could look through to her soul. It seemed, strangely, that she had been waiting for ever to hear those words from him.

'I...' In the darkened room her shadowed face revealed all that she felt, for better or worse. There was no hiding it. Her lips were parted and her eyes explored his face.

The tension hung between them like something tangible. Slowly Jan closed her eyes in acquiescence, swaying slightly towards him, her legs weak. She did not have to say anything.

When he reached forward and began to undo the tiny buttons on the front of her wet blouse he was shaking so much that she insinuated her hands under his to help him. She was shivering, but not with cold, for the first time in her life, as at last his fingers found her sensitized skin.

'For a surgeon, you're very inept,' she whispered, laughing softly with anticipation as he eased the wet garment off her shoulders with sensual, stroking movements that made her murmur with pleasure. As he kissed her neck and tickled her sensitive earlobe with the tip of his tongue his hands moved up her back to unclip the tiny lace bra that she wore, exposing her breasts to the warm, caressing air of the closed room. With an easy movement she took it off and let it drop to the floor.

'See if you can do any better,' he murmured challengingly, smiling at her with a kind of triumph. Capturing her hands, he moved them to the buttons of his clinging shirt. Aware of his urgency, she began to fumble with them, making a mess of it with uncoordinated movements.

'Shall I help?' He whispered the words against her ear. 'Please.'

They did not speak as he took off his shirt and unbuckled the belt of his pants. Drawing her against him, he put her hands on his hips so that she could ease his clothing from his body and feel his sexual arousal firmly against her. Trembling, she closed her eyes as she peeled the clinging linen from his taut body until he was able to step out of it.

He lifted her up. 'Don't shut your eyes, Jan.'

Then he swung her up into his arms, his breathing ragged. Shaking uncontrollably, he lowered her onto the wide, capacious horsehair sofa that was in the room. It was hard, unyielding against her back, the leather cover sticking to her damp skin. 'So this is what the sofa is for,' Jan mused through the haze of her passion. 'It's for making love on. I've always wondered…'

Looking at him surreptitiously through her lashes and her tangled hair, which fell over her forehead, she helped him to finish undressing her.

'Look at me, Jan.' He whispered the words as he lay down with her, his body partly covering hers. The exultant desire that blazed on his face as she looked at him matched the emotion that was engulfing her like a tide.

'Oh, Gerard…' She lifted her mouth to his, and her trembling hands touched his hair, then moved to his nape to pull him closer to her. 'Please…'

Without preamble, her body arched to meet his touch when his hand found the soft inner skin of her thighs, and she cried out when she felt his fingers gently entering her body. They were both impatient, matched in desire, in need.

'Please….' she whispered again.

As a relentless tide of pure pleasure mounted in her at his caressing touch, she knew that he would take precautions to protect her. It was obvious that he had planned to be here like this. She ought to mind, she ought to be angry, but her need was greater.

In every sense of the word, he was taking possession of her—utterly and completely. Gradually, competently, losing himself in her pleasure and murmuring incoherently, he brought her to the edge of ecstasy.

Crying out, she gripped his shoulders and dug her nails into his firm flesh. When he moved over her she welcomed his weight on her. When he entered her there was nothing else in the world but him… Nothing else mattered, other than the most exquisite pleasure she had ever known. Quietly she began to laugh and to sob at the same time...

'I can't leave you alone all night.' The words filtered through to Jan as she lay with her limbs entwined with Gerard's, her head beside his on a cushion. At last, satiated for now, they waited for the tumultuous emotions to subside and for their breathing to return to normal.

'Don't go, then,' she whispered back.

They were both slippery with sweat. Little runnels of moisture ran down between her breasts. As moments passed she felt peace stealing over her, an exquisite joy of fulfillment as though for a precious interval time had stood still for them. As fading sunlight filtered through the shutters she felt him gradually relax and fall into an exhausted sleep. I'll close my eyes too, she thought, just for a few minutes.

The whining of Pansy woke her with a jerk. The sitting room was almost dark. Beside her on the sofa Gerard still slept so deeply that she suspected he had not had a decent sleep for days, and compassion for him engulfed her. Since the storm there must have been little time for rest.

In the half-light his face was peaceful, almost boyish in repose. She allowed her gaze to go over him, imprinting his image on her memory. For her his love-making had been a revelation. He had seemed to know her needs instinctively, what she had been thinking and feeling. What now? It was as though she had spoken the question aloud because now it presented itself to her as a dilemma. They had to work together when the attraction, the recollection of this time, would be with them constantly.

When the dog whined again she carefully extricated herself from Gerard's embrace and inched herself away from him off the sofa, trying not to wake him.

'Hullo, Pansy,' she whispered in the hall. 'Good dog.' Carefully she closed the sitting-room door behind her and ran up to her room for a robe. In moments she was under the shower, soaping her body and washing her hair, revelling in the memory of his touch on her.

Their love-making had been like a madness, a crazy abandonment. Perhaps I am mad, Jan told herself. In a short time she would be gone from the island again, and even when she came back to Manara—if they could keep it— she would have no reason to see Gerard de Prescy. What was that he had said to Etienne? He took his pleasure where he found it... Yes, that was what he had said. Well, perhaps they were two of a kind because that was what she had done, wasn't it? Emotionally, she was not involved, she told herself emphatically.

Jan applied talcum powder and a light, tangy cologne, before dressing in a casual shift dress and brushing out her wet hair. From the linen cupboard she took a towelling robe that belonged to her father and, quietly entering the sitting room again, laid it over the recumbent man. He had not moved from the position in which she had left him. Then she let out the dog for a few minutes, before calling her into the kitchen and giving her a dish of water.

'You must be hungry, eh?' she said to the attentive canine as she prepared food in the kitchen. 'I'll have to wait until your master wakes up to find out what he's brought for you.'

The simple meal of rice, black-eyed beans and spiced fish was almost finished when Gerard came to stand in the doorway, clad in the robe, his hair tousled. 'Hi,' he said, running a hand through his hair. 'Could I use your shower?' The smile he gave her was lazy, a veiled light of assessment in his eyes as he looked at her.

'Yes...of course.' She directed him to the bathroom. 'I...I've cooked us something to eat. I assumed you would be hungry.' Flushing a little, she found herself unable to sustain eye contact for more than a few seconds.

'That's great. Do you still mind if I stay the night?' He lounged against the doorframe, as though he asked that question all the time.

'No... No...'

'For once I have a free night. I'm on call from noon tomorrow for the rest of the weekend. It's about time I caught up on some sleep.' With another lazy smile, he left her.

Later that night she lay with him again—in her bed this time, where he was a protective presence. With him there Jan allowed herself to think more clearly about the past...and about her own future. When she shifted slightly she came into contact with his warm skin as he slept beside her, a touch that kept her demons, as she often thought of them, from affecting her too much. It was nice to have him there. She smiled into the darkness.

They had made love again, more slowly this time but no less explosively. Again she got the impression that he had not made love to a woman for quite a long time. His hunger for her had had a quality of urgency to it that was quite revealing.

As they had eaten the simple supper earlier, Gerard had said, 'Tell me about Dr. Clairmont, the younger.' Hesitant at first, Jan had talked about the events around her break-up with John. It had been a cathartic experience to talk about it to someone who had not known either of them then, a relative stranger.

What she had not been able to tell him were the words that John had shouted at her after he had been reprimanded by his senior staff surgeon, following the operation where their patient had almost died.

'You bitch!' he had shouted at her, his face red, his eyes bulging with anger as he had jabbed a finger threateningly at her face. 'You bitch! You set me up!'

'No...' she had protested, terrified. 'You set yourself up.

If the patient had died it would be a coroner's case... There could be a law suit... Your name would be in the newspapers...'

He had said other things, awful, hurtful things, and she had thought, up to then, that he had loved her. Now she thought about those words, which at the time had badly undermined her confidence in herself as a woman. Now, with this man beside her, they somehow seemed to have less power to hurt her. Gerard was an entirely different type of man.

Jan shifted carefully so that she could put her cheek against his warm back, which was turned away from her.

'Awake?' he said huskily, turning slowly to her, putting an arm over her and smoothing a hand down over her hip before moving so that their bodies touched.

'Yes.'

Although refreshed by sleep, they were both still tired. Yet there were questions in Jan's mind about him. She had told him a fair amount about herself, but he had said little about himself.

'You said you had been married once,' she began, blurting out the question that had been in her mind for the last few hours. 'Are you divorced?'

No,' he said evenly. 'My wife died...about two and a half years ago.'

'Oh...'

'That's why I'm here in St. Bonar. She wanted to come back here when she knew she was sick, because she was born here.' His voice was expressionless.

'I'm sorry, Gerard,' she said softly.

'Why should you be sorry?' he said, somewhat brusquely. 'It has nothing to do with you.'

Jan stiffened within the circle of his arms. This was not, perhaps, the time or the place to talk about his wife, yet she had needed to know.

When they made love again, and she gave herself up mindlessly to the intense pleasure he gave her, she nonetheless felt a desperation in him as he took his own pleasure from her body. She also thought she detected a withdrawal in him, an almost imperceptible pulling back from her.

CHAPTER NINE

IT WAS a pleasant surprise on Monday morning to discover that the itinerant community nurse, Anne, would come to Eden Bay at least twice a week to help Jan with the baby clinic, among other things, when infants and very young children were brought by their mothers for check-ups. The nurse was already there when Jan arrived.

'Hello, pleased to meet you. I'm Anne.' The nurse, a local woman, who appeared to be in her thirties, introduced herself when Jan entered the clinic.

'Hi. It's good to see you.' Jan smiled and dumped her bag beside the desk in the office, quickly tidying her wind-blown hair. They shook hands.

'Sorry I haven't been here before. Things have been crazy. Like a cup o' coffee?'

'I would...thanks.'

Anne began to fill her in on the more intricate details of the routine clinics, which would resume now that some of the storm damage had been cleared up. It was soon obvious that they were going to get along like the proverbial house on fire.

'Then I'll show you how to set up for the baby clinic, Dr Newsome. There are scales for weighing the babies, others for the young kids, and so on.' The nurse chatted, busying herself making coffee.

'Mothers have health record cards for each of their kids. They bring the cards in when they come and we fill them in, then if they move to another area or go to hospital they take the cards with them. It's simple, but it works. Of course, we keep a few basic records here too...mainly vaccination records.'

'That sounds sensible,' Jan commented. 'I'm sorry I'm only here temporarily. It's all so interesting and I'm just beginning to feel like I belong.'

'Well, you could always stay.' Anne laughed, and handed her a cup of coffee. 'This place isn't exactly over-supplied with doctors. I've been driving all over the island, going where I've been needed most, in the past two weeks. Dr Gerard said you would be able to cope here.' Her teeth gleamed in her dark, friendly face as she smiled.

Oh, did he? Jan thought, the mention of Gerard making her hold her breath for a moment in consternation. Their passionate coming together had been like a fantasy interlude, an experience that now seemed decidedly unreal—yet it had happened. Jan sipped her coffee, recalling their parting on Saturday when he had left her to return to Fort Roche.

There had been an almost unbearable sexual tension between them that, paradoxically, had been enhanced rather than dimmed by its recent consummation. There had been a prickliness, too, and a drawing back on his part that she had experienced the night before. Just as well, she had thought defensively. This is just a brief interlude in my life. When they had parted he had kissed her gently. 'See you at work, Jan, some time next week. I'll pick up the dog in a day or two.'

In spite of her assertions, she had felt lonely when he had gone. On the same afternoon she had picked up her father from the hospital, and she was pleased to see he had benefited from the enforced rest. So far, all was well there. Now they had to wait for the biopsy results.

'I think Dr Gerard would love to have you here permanently so if you decide not to go back to the States there would always be a job for you here.' The nurse was looking at her astutely, perhaps having read her troubled thoughts and maybe guessed how she had spent part of the weekend. She wasn't exactly good at subterfuge. 'What do you think of him, by the way?'

'He's a very good doctor, from what I've seen,' Jan said truthfully. The nurse waited. 'And he's an unusual...very attractive man.' She smiled apologetically at the admission.

Anne laughed. 'You can say that again! He's a real sexy beast. If ever a man needed a good woman, he does.'

'What do you mean?'

'Well, I don't want to gossip, but he's such a nice person and he's had an awful time with his wife. She died, you know, about two years ago. She had a lung cancer, which was a bit of a mystery when she presented with it because she had never smoked. Turned out it was a secondary tumor, from a very small breast tumor that didn't show up at first on a mammogram. It was found too late and there was nothing they could do for her.'

'How awful.'

'Yeah, it was. They were living in the States at the time. She wanted to come back here to die, so they came. She was one of the Rennies, you see, the hotel people. Isobel Rennie. Of course, she had been sent away after the age of thirteen to boarding school in England, then to Switzerland, but she spent holidays here,' the nurse said sadly, as though she were recounting a saga that she had heard and repeated many times, as probably she had. 'It was tragic. She was the love of his life. She had everything...beauty, brains, breeding, money, you name it...'

'Isobel Rennie.' Jan breathed the name. 'I knew of her...'

'You would have done,' Anne confirmed. 'It was her grandfather that opened the first tourist hotel up on the north-west coast years ago, then her dad took over, then her brothers. They have hotels, first-class ones, all over the Caribbean now. Isobel worked for the hotel chain as well.'

'Yes, I remember now.' Jan murmured, thinking of pictures she had seen of Isobel Rennie in society magazines and in local newspapers—a tall, leggy blonde. 'Did they have children?'

'No, they never did. Just as well, I expect. Well...' Anne looked at her wrist-watch. 'Back to work! If ever a man needed a woman, he does! But he would never admit it. I'm not a gossip, you know, Dr Newsome. It's just that I like the man so much.'

When they began to get organized for work, Jan forced her mind away from Gerard and from Manara. At least her dad would be all right. Theresa, the housekeeper, and her daughter would, between them, keep a subtle eye on him and telephone her if anything did not seem right.

The mothers came in unprecedented numbers because they had discovered that the consultation with her was free. Although hospital and clinic care for children was free with a nurse, a visit to a pediatrician or other doctor for routine care was not free. The fee was beyond the pockets of ordinary working people. Jan took great pleasure in providing them with a very useful service.

As the day wore on she saw a number of older children who suffered from tuberculosis and several toddlers who had kwashiorkor, the protein deficiency syndrome that she had only read about in textbooks on tropical diseases. Because Gerard had warned her about it, she was particularly on the lookout for it. There had been no mistaking it. It was a type of malnutrition, common when the mother had a new baby and the toddler was suddenly deprived of breast milk.

With only a quick break for lunch, the clinic was over before Jan realized how many hours had gone by. She had enjoyed every minute of it—the people were friendly and welcoming, quick to smile. Also, in a quiet way, they thoroughly appreciated everything she did for them, taking nothing for granted.

After the last patient had gone Anne rushed around, clearing up and putting everything in order. 'I'm not sure at the moment whether I or Dr Gerard will be here with you tomorrow, Dr Newsome,' she said, as she prepared to go out the door, leaving Jan to finish writing up a few records and to lock up. 'I expect Dr Gerard will telephone before you shut up shop.'

'All right, Anne. It's been a great day.'

The telephone rang as she was making herself tea after she had finished her record charts.

'Eden Bay clinic,' she answered. 'Dr Newsome speaking.'

'Hello, Jan. How are you?' There was no mistaking Gerard's deep voice, with its West Indian twang.

'I...um...I've had a really good day.' Jan found herself stammering a little. 'Very busy, but satisfying. The kids are really delightful. And...um...the nurse was here, of course.'

'Great!' he said. 'I'm glad you enjoyed it. I'm at Manara right now. The visiting surgeons were here, looking around, for a short while. They were mainly interested in the land. I thought I would come to the clinic to discuss it with you, then come back here to get Pansy.'

'Oh...' That was quick work, Jan decided, sounding dubious. 'Did my father know they were coming?'

'We telephoned him. They decided on the spur of the moment this morning that they would like to have a look at it.'

'Oh...' she said again, strangely bereft of words.

'I'll see you in a short while.'

Jan washed her face in the sink of the washroom, then brushed her hair and made an effort to render herself more presentable by adding a little make-up. The sun had turned her face to a soft honey colour, tinged now with pink from the exertion of work. Even though the interior of the clinic was pleasantly warm, cooled by the ceiling fans, she was sweating from effort and the fact that she was wearing a long-sleeved shirt and cotton trousers under her white lab coat to guard against mosquito bites.

There was an uneasy feeling in the back of her mind that perhaps Gerard had seduced her in more ways than one—or hoped that he had. Maybe he hoped that his love-making had softened her stance over Manara. She thought then of Isobel Rennie, who had been, by reputation, a member of the so-called island jet-set. She would have been, Jan calculated, at least five years older than she was herself.

The clinic had a small verandah at the back that overlooked the sweeping view of the sea and the village, which seemed to tumble in a haphazard fashion down the hill to the beach. Jan stood out there to sip the very welcome tea.

Her heart gave an uncomfortable lurch of anticipation when she heard a car climbing the hill, and she went inside quickly to rinse her cup and wash her hands. If he thought she was going to be easily persuaded to sell her property then he could think again, she reasoned firmly.

However, when the car came to a halt right outside the door of the clinic, instead of in the parking spaces under the shade of the calabash tree, she knew that it was not Gerard and that she was needed urgently. Wiping her wet hands on a towel, she went to the door.

'Oh, thank God! We had no idea what we would find here. We were directed up here by someone down in the village.' The words were spoken by one of three pale, late-middle-aged women, all dressed in sturdy shorts and T-shirts, who had crowded through the doorway. They were not the kind of shorts and T-shirts that one might wear on a beach.

'Are you a doctor?' another one of them asked in a booming, authoritative voice that had a southern American twang.

'Yes, I am,' Jan answered. 'What can I do for you?'

'Thank God!' one of the other woman reiterated. 'Our friend in the car isn't well. We think she may be suffering from the heat. We've been doing some walking in the hills. We've overdone it, I think, walking in the heat of the day. Bloody silly of us, really.'

They looked like a trio of university professors, Jan surmised, with their no-nonsense short, iron-gray hair, the functional clothing and hiking boots. No doubt they would have backpacks in the car. They all had American accents.

'Are we ever glad to see you! ' the third woman chipped in. 'A touch of civilization! We figured we wouldn't make it back to the hotel...she's been vomiting, you see. Needs fluids, no doubt, but can't keep anything down. Have you got a wheelchair or something we could put her in? I don't think she could walk in here.'

'We think she's on the verge of collapse,' the first speaker stated in a very businesslike fashion.

Somewhat bemused by this sudden change in clientele, Jan indicated a folded wheelchair which was kept behind the door. 'Please take this,' she offered, hauling it out. 'How far are you from your hotel?' It was not necessary to ask if they were tourists.

'Oh, a long way. We're way up in the north of the island, staying at the Carlyle at Dolphin Bay. What we didn't think enough about was that there would be a lot of storm damage in the rain forests. The walking was harder going than we thought it would be.'

That remark reminded Jan sharply of Gerard de Prescy and the irritation he had shown her when she had arrived on the island and he had chased after her on horseback. Now the positions were reversed as she looked at this group of women, feeling a measure of irritation tempering her concern. They should have known better.

'That's quite a way,' Jan agreed, following them out smartly to the car, where another woman of the same ilk was lying on the back seat.

'We've got help, Millie,' one of the others practically shouted at the recumbent figure. 'Here's a wheelchair for you, dear.'

With impressive efficiency and co-ordination of purpose, the three women managed to haul their friend out of the car and into the wheelchair, while Jan did some sizing up of her own.

'Does she have diabetes?' she queried the efficient friends. 'Or a history of any heart problems?' Before making a diagnosis of heat exhaustion, which it appeared to be, she would have to eliminate a few other possibilities common to the late middle aged as soon as possible.

'No, nothing like that. She's in great shape normally. I'm Pat, by the way.' The woman took Jan's hand in a decisive grasp. 'And this is Wilma, that's Alice…and this is poor Millie. Would you believe it—her name's Strong? Millie Strong.' She gave a bark of laughter, in which the others joined. Even Millie managed a weak smile as she slumped sideways in the chair. Jan could see that she looked ill. Her skin had a yellowish tinge and her eyes appeared sunken.

'I'm Dr Newsome. Get her inside quickly,' Jan said, trying to take command of the situation and wondering whether she had been wrong in her supposition that they were university professors. Perhaps they were in the military.

If the situation had not been so potentially serious, she might have given way to the amusement that bubbled up inside her as the women, in their incongruous hiking boots, maneuvered their friend into the interior of the clinic and heaved her onto an examination table. While they did that

Jan quickly plugged in two small electric fans, directing the flow of cool air over the examination table.

'Take it easy, Millie,' the one called Alice commanded. 'You're OK now.'

'She's all yours, Doctor,' Wilma said. With that, they all flattened themselves back against the walls of the small examination room to give her space to work. 'You don't mind if we stay, do you? Millie would like us to be with her.'

Unable to suppress a smile, Jan shook her head and advanced on her patient with the basic tools of her trade in her hands. 'No,' she said. 'I expect you're right about the heat. It's probably heat exhaustion so I want to take her temperature first, then her pulse rate and blood pressure. Then I shall want a specimen of your urine, Millie, if you can manage it.' Turning to the patient, Jan addressed her directly for the first time.

Millie nodded weakly. 'I'll try,' she whispered.

'She's dehydrated,' one of the others said. 'Couldn't keep any fluids down when she should have been drinking. Her salt level will be down too, won't it, Doctor?'

'Yes, I expect it will, ' Jan said, taking Millie's temperature. 'I want the urine to test for salt content, which will help to make the diagnosis. I shall want to give her some intravenous saline and possibly some dextrose as well. You'll have to stay here for quite a while.'

'Great stuff, Doctor! Thank God we found you. This is a little pocket of civilization in the land of the infidel, you might say.'

'Hardly the infidel, Wilma. There are churches all over the place,' Pat chided her.

'Well, you know what I mean.'

Managing to shut her mind to the background badinage, which she suspected disguised a high level of anxiety, Jan concentrated on her patient, who was moving her head rest-lessly from side to side.

The temperature was only a little above normal, but the pulse rate was very rapid, as Jan had thought it would be. The skin was pale, moist and cool to the touch, which in-dicated that the sick woman was still capable of sweating. In some types of pyrexia all sweating stopped, which was a dangerous sign. Millie Strong looked exhausted, not like someone who had just enjoyed a holiday at a beach hotel.

'Is this the first day you've been out walking?' Jan said, addressing herself to the friends—building up a picture in her mind of what might have happened.

'No, we've been out for the last four days for several hours each day,' someone answered. 'We tried not to overdo it, but obviously we have.'

There was no need for Jan to tell them they were stu-pid—they obviously knew it themselves now. When she checked the patient's blood pressure she found it to be lower than normal. Carefully, she listened to Millie's heart with her stethoscope. Apart from the rapid rate, it sounded normal.

'How are you feeling, Millie?' she said gently. 'Can you tell me what your symptoms are?'

'I feel awful,' Millie said softly. 'Terrible head-ache...nauseated...I did vomit earlier. My muscles hurt too.'

'Have you been passing urine all right today? The same amount as usual?' As Jan questioned her patient she jotted down her findings on a sheet of paper attached to a clip-board.

'Well...no. Some, but not as much, I think. I feel so dizzy. I hurt all over.'

Suddenly Jan felt a stab of recognition. Could this be dengue fever? There were the muscle pains, the severe fron-tal headache. No. She didn't think so, really. The temper-

ature was not high enough, the patient not sufficiently febrile. Not that she had ever seen a case of dengue, in the
early stage or otherwise.

'Do you have any visual disturbances, Millie?' Jan queried urgently, bending close to her patient so that she could
hear the whispered responses. 'Like spots before the eyes?
And do you hear any ringing in the ears? This is very important.'

'Yes…yes…I do… Black spots, like rain. A ringing in
my ears…yes…sometimes,' Millie confirmed, her eyes
closing wearily.

Jan felt herself relax. Heat exhaustion she could cope
with. Probably she could cope with dengue also, but she
would rather not until she had first seen a case with some
other doctor in attendance.

'Millie, I am going to sit you on a bedpan to get a specimen of your urine so that I can test it. Then I'm going to
start you on intravenous saline—salt solution—as the level
of salt in your blood is probably depleted.'

In deference to the need for privacy by their friend, the
trio of women trooped out of the room. 'We'll be back,
Millie. Hang in there, gal!'

Her patient could only produce a few drops of urine, just
about enough for the test that would reveal the salt content.
That in itself more or less clinched the diagnosis, Jan considered, weighing up the pros and cons.

She would do the test after she had started an intravenous
infusion of the salt solution, normal saline, to get the
woman rehydrated as quickly as possible. There could be
kidney and brain damage with this condition, although Jan
did not think that her case was of the most serious nature.
However, she was not going to take chances of any sort.

When she had the intravenous line in and the fluid running, she called the other women back in. 'Would you stay
with her while I do a test?'

'Yes,' they chorused, relieved perhaps of collective guilt by being able to do something to help.

As Jan took the urine sample out to the laboratory area to do the test, she considered what else she would do. She would run half a liter of saline fairly quickly into the woman's veins, then slow it down somewhat over the next hour. She made up her mind to run in a pack of intravenous plasma as well to raise the blood volume. They kept two packs of fresh plasma in the refrigerator. This case proved how vital it was never to run out of essential stock. Cases which were not initially potentially life-threatening could become so if the right treatment was not on hand.

The urine contained no salt. As Jan left the laboratory area she heard Gerard's car come to a halt under the calabash tree, and she went out to meet him, wanting to tell him in privacy about the case. At least she could get a second opinion. And thank God they had a patient between them to temper the awkwardness of this first meeting after their tumultuous coupling.

'Hi,' he said, getting out of the car slowly and stretching his tall frame as though he were infinitely weary. To Jan he looked almost as exhausted as when she had first set eyes on him. 'How have you been? Got trouble here?' He nodded towards the parked car. His light shirt was streaked with moisture, and a stubble of beard darkened his face. Perhaps he had been up all night, operating, Jan speculated.

'I'm fine,' Jan said, brushing hair out of her eyes. She suddenly felt self-conscious, remembering how he had looked without clothes, his tanned skin glistening with sweat, his lithe body unselfconsciously displayed. For a moment he was very still, and she knew without doubt that he was thinking exactly the same thoughts about her...

'It's not exactly trouble,' she added quickly. 'A woman—a tourist—with heat exhaustion, I think.' Briefly she told him about the case, asking if he would mind checking Millie Strong.

'Sure,' he agreed, bending to lift out a metal packing case from his car. 'I've brought some supplies for the women's clinic on Thursday—the new clinic we're setting up. It's stuff for the tests themselves and for the lab tests. I have some things to discuss with you concerning that.'

'I see.'

'Don McLean wants us to do hepatitis B tests on all the women of child-bearing age as well so the negative ones can be vaccinated as soon as possible. He's sent out notices.' He sounded very businesslike, and Jan was relieved. 'Sorry it's such short notice for you. We were waiting for these supplies to come from the States—they just arrived this morning. We've got a hospital and a major drug company to sponsor our work until we can really get it going.'

'That's great,' Jan said, wondering how she was going to cope on her own.

As though reading her mind, he went on, 'I'll be here with you, and I hope the nurse will be here too. Things have been hectic for me, otherwise I would have called to explain. We can discuss it at Manara later, if you don't mind.'

'That's fine,' she said. As he followed her she could sense that he had no intention of letting personal matters interfere with work while he was actually on the job.

'I want to put some of these supplies in the refrigerator,' he said, striding toward the clinic entrance, 'then I'll be happy to take a look at your patient.'

'Thanks.' Jan lingered in the sunshine for a few minutes. These days she was spending too much time inside.

Two hours later Millie Strong lay peacefully sleeping, with the remainder of the I.V. fluid dripping in slowly, while her friends were ensconced on the clinic verandah, supplied by Jan with cool drinks. Gerard was talking to them. Jan could hear his deep voice and snatches of laughter from the women, who had relaxed considerably. It was obvious that he could be a very charming host, and he was now playing the part very well. No doubt he had had plenty of experience with the Rennie family...

Jan stood by her patient, adjusting the rate of flow on the I.V. line. It was imperative that she should not overdo things and give too much fluid too quickly. Several times she had checked that her patient was able to pass urine and that her kidneys had not been damaged by her earlier dehydration. It was certainly dangerous to overload someone with fluid if they could not eliminate what was not required by the body.

'Perfect, Dr Newsome,' Gerard had said, for the benefit of the woman's friends, before he had started to chat to them. A niggle of annoyance and tension tempered her earlier buoyant mood.

Carefully she made notes on the input and output chart. Everything had to be written in duplicate so that she could send a copy with the patient to be read by the doctor who would be taking over. Millie Strong had elected to return to the hotel, rather than be admitted to the Fort Roche hospital for a night or two.

Gerard, having agreed with Jan's diagnosis, had arranged special transport for Millie Strong. They were waiting for a private ambulance to come from the north part of the island, from the hotel area, where two doctors serviced the hotel guests as well as running local practices. The 'ambulance' was, Jan had been told, a converted van in which patients could be accommodated on a stretcher. Millie Strong would be more comfortable in that than in the cramped car in which she had arrived.

'The only other thing I would suggest,' Gerard said just behind her, 'is that I take a blood sample to the epidemiology lab in Fort Roche. They can do a test there to rule out dengue fever. I'm pretty sure that what she's suffering from *is* heat exhaustion, but it would be stupid not to do the other test while we have her here.'

In moments he had located the necessary test tubes and syringes for the blood tests and had drawn some blood from the rubber port in the I.V. line, all very quickly and efficiently. Millie Strong's three friends stood admiringly in the doorway.

When they heard the engine of the ambulance-cum-van, laboring up the hill, he shook hands all round and said, 'It was a pleasure to meet you all.'

'So it's been a good day?' Gerard said, when the cool of dusk and a light breeze from the sea made the clinic garden into an oasis of tranquillity just as they were leaving.

They were standing under the tree where the bougainvillea had twisted itself in parasitic fashion high on the trunk, and the bright petals wafted to the ground, loosened by the wind. The ephemeral nature of their beauty added a poignancy to the scene as Jan stepped on them to get to her car. '''*Plus ça change, c'est plus la même chose*.''' Jan muttered the words as the petals floated round her.

'Yes, a very good day,' she said aloud. Now that they were alone, the actuality of what had happened on the weekend seemed to stand between them.

'Jan...I feel I ought to say how much I enjoyed...being with you Friday night.' His voice was husky. 'I hope it won't affect the good working relationship that we seem to be developing.'

'I don't think it will.' Color suffused her face.

'I hope, also, that it won't be...an isolated incident.' His voice was so low that she scarcely heard him, as though he were frightened that the trees would have ears. Information on the island certainly spread quickly. She could not meet his eyes.

'I know,' he went on, 'that you won't be on St Bonar very long, that there's no question of it being permanent...' They stood close and Jan felt the tension rising. 'I hope you can accept me in the spirit...in which I am offering myself.'

Looking at him then, Jan could see that he was very serious. Since she had last seen him, his face had become paler, strained.

'You mean that you would like me to be your mistress, or whatever the current word is, for the time that I'm on the island?' A tumult of emotion filled her with confusion and the charged atmosphere intensified.

'Yes,' he answered, his voice low.

How incongruous this was, Jan thought, looking around wildly. Anyone watching them might think they were having a professional conversation.

'Is this what you usually do with visiting female doctors?' she said hotly, both flattered and angry.

'No. Those are very few and far between. I haven't made love to a woman for...about two years.'

'Since your wife...?'

'Yes. Perhaps Anne told you about her? She likes to chatter.'

Jan nodded, biting her lip and looking away from him.

'I loved her,' he said, his voice barely audible. 'Isobel...loved life, she was so full of fun. It seemed impossible that she would die, but she did. She faded away like a flower, then she was gone.'

Mauve pieces of bougainvillea floated around them, oddly echoing the metaphor he had chosen. 'Is that why you stay on St Bonar—to be near the memory of her?'

'Perhaps. The people here need me, all the skills that I have to offer. That's one of its many charms.'

For moments they stood silently. Then he reached forward and stroked her cheek. 'Jan...' he said softly.

'Don't...' She jerked her head away.

'The visiting surgeons do not think that Manara is suitable for their purposes,' he said, addressing her bent head. 'It's too far away from Fort Roche and the airport. But I want it, Jan. I want it for myself. Will you let me have it?'

'You think,' she said, her eyes blazing, 'that I'm a sexually frustrated career-woman who will capitulate about the sale of my house if you—?'

'No!' He cut her off. 'Look at this!' He held out his arms in front of him. She could see that his hands were shaking.

With a muffled cry, she ran from him to her car. She slammed the door and started the engine, not looking at him. Danger signals seemed to be going off in her brain. She was in danger of breaking her own rules of not getting involved. One thing he had done for her—John Clairmont was rapidly receding from her life.

She drove away, without looking back. What she did not want him to see were her own trembling hands.

Jack Newsome was sleeping on the verandah when Jan got back to Manara, under some sort of contraption that he had rigged up with mosquito netting. Jan tiptoed past, after ensuring that he was all right, then she ran up to her room. There was noise and muffled radio music coming from the kitchen, where the housekeeper and her daughter were preparing supper. Pansy was there too, and her deep bark added to the noise. Gerard was following her and would soon be there. Her father, no doubt, would invite him to supper.

After undressing hastily, Jan wrapped herself in a large towel and crossed the wide landing to the bathroom to have a shower. The cool water calmed her churning thoughts. Yes, she wanted Gerard de Prescy, wanted to be his lover—she admitted it. But, like all women, she knew that she was capable of being hurt and was frightened of it, frightened of getting into a situation that she could not control. Was he using her?

Back in her room she began to towel herself dry. When there was a tap on her door she called out, 'Just a minute!' It would be Theresa, confirming how many there would be for supper.

Gerard stood there when she opened the door. The expression on his face was serious, brooding. Through the open neck of his shirt she could see the dark, rough hairs of his chest. Her eyes rested there and on the pulse in his neck. 'May I come in?' he said.

With her heart beating wildly, she was poised for flight. She wanted to shout at him to go away, but wanted him at the same time. What on earth would her father think? Or the housekeeper? And what was happening to her?

Instead, she stepped aside to let him enter, and watched him turn the old iron key in the lock of the mahogany door. Swallowing nervously, she waited while he turned to her. His eyes seemed to devour her and time stood still. When he reached forward to ease the towel from her body she did not resist, letting it fall.

'My God...Jan!' he muttered, pulling her into his arms. Their mouths came together, blindly searching, and she put her arms up around his neck, standing on tiptoe to get close to him. In moments they were on her bed, her hands searching beneath his clothing.

'Live with me, Jan,' he muttered urgently. 'Come to live with me in Fort Roche...'

'I can't. I have to be here with my father.'

'He has to leave here. He must.'

'Don't talk...'

When he entered her the cry she gave was muffled by his demanding mouth on hers...

CHAPTER TEN

JACK NEWSOME didn't seem to notice that Jan was flushed and abstracted when she joined him and Gerard a little late to eat a simple supper on the verandah. He was talking animatedly to the other man about island affairs. Neither did he appear to notice that she said very little throughout the meal.

When they had finished eating, Jan got up and took a cup of coffee along the verandah away from them. They could not go on like this, she and Gerard, she thought wildly, staring out over the gardens with unfocused eyes. She was getting far too involved with him—an understatement, if ever there was one. It was madness. That he had asked her to live with him when they hardly knew each other was also incredible. What on earth did he think her father would do, here alone? Of course, he had been essentially alone before, but that had been before he'd had a diagnosis pinned to his ill-health.

Neither could she understand her own behaviour. She had entered into an affair with him as though it were perfectly natural, as though she had been waiting to do just that...

A presence made itself felt behind her—a tingling awareness, as though someone had actually touched her.

'I forgot to ask you earlier,' Gerard said, coming to stand at ease beside her, holding a cup of coffee, 'if you would mind coming to Fort Roche on Sunday for an hour or two to teach the technicians about the tests for the human papilloma virus. Then they would be ready for our women's clinic specimens when they come in. I know it's one of your days off but there just isn't any other opportunity. You'll be going back to the States before we know it.'

'I can do that,' Jan said, making a show of sipping her coffee.

'Don McLean wants us to do finger-prick tests for blood sugar on all those women too,' he went on. 'Diabetes is one of the most common chronic diseases here, so we might as well take the opportunity to test for it too, plus a hemoglobin test on each woman to rule out anemia.' He spoke matter-of-factly, as though they had not been in each other's arms scarcely an hour before.

'We're going to be busy,' Jan forced herself to say. 'I'm looking forward to it.'

'We want to do as much in preventative care as we can,' he said. 'It's cheaper in the long run, and saves a lot of unnecessary suffering.'

'Yes.'

Jack Newsome got up to go inside, leaving them alone, and Jan came to a decision. Before she could speak Gerard was talking again.

'Do you remember when we first met I mentioned I might be related to the Daviot family?'

'Yes.'

'I heard from Father Jessop a few days ago about my family history,' he said. 'He's been doing research for me in France and in Martinique…and here. It seems that I am related to the Daviot family.' When he turned to her, compelling her to look at him, there was a light of something like triumph in his face—an excitement, a strange happiness.

Jan was bewildered. 'How? I thought I knew quite a lot about the Daviot family of France. I don't believe it.'

'Not them exactly. My connection is through Manara…Manara, the slave woman.'

Jan felt her lips parting in amazement. They stood si-

lently, looking at each other, as though caught in that familiar time warp that she often felt at Manara, where the
events of the past somehow reached forward to touch them
in the present.

With a flutter of wings, breaking the silence, a pair of
mourning doves flew from the lawn to the top of a casua-
rina tree and began their plaintive calling. A shiver went
through Jan.

'I don't believe it,' she whispered, staring at him. But
she did believe it...yes, she did. His dark eyes smoldered
with a look of triumph.

'This is my birthright,' he said. 'If I have this land, a
kind of justice will have been done. Manara had a daughter,
Belle, who did not die in the cholera epidemic. She and a
brother escaped to France with their father. He left them
there, before coming back to St Bonar, where he died. Belle
was my great-great-grandmother. Henri Daviot left her
some of this land, but because she was an illegitimate child,
as well as a half-caste, the law of the time on St Bonar
would not allow her to inherit.'

'It's incredible,' Jan said, mesmerized by the story. 'How
can I believe it?'

'Father Jessop will tell you. He has documents. Some of
the family subsequently moved from France to Martinique.'

It was as though time had shifted. The tenuous hold of
the Newsome family on this land had shifted. It was as
though a question from the past had been answered...

Pansy came out to the verandah. They watched her flop
down on the coconut matting. Gerard reached forward to
touch Jan's arm.

'I must go. Call me if you need anything...or want to
talk, otherwise I'll see you tomorrow at the clinic if there's
nothing urgent at the hospital.'

'Wait!' Jan tuned to face him. 'I think it would be better
if you did not concern yourself any more with our financial

affairs until we've decided that we definitely want to sell.'
The words came out in a rush. 'Also, I...I think it would
be better if we were to keep our relationship strictly professional from now on.'

A conviction had been growing in her that his pursuit of
her, their passionate physical contact, had been part of his
need to break down her defences regarding the property. It
was a chance she could not take. Bit by bit she was losing
control and now it was time to back off. Besides, it was
difficult for her to trust a man at the moment, and she was
frightened.

As she faced him stiffly a look of muted shock passed
over his face. 'If that's what you want,' he said after a
moment, his voice flat.

'Yes, it is.'

'All right. I'm very sorry,' he said softly. 'Goodbye, Jan.
I'll see myself out.'

Jan listened to his footsteps as he walked away from her
through the quiet house, the dog following. She listened to
his voice as he said goodbye to her father. Then there was
the sound of his car, driving away up the track. Avoiding
her father, Jan ran up to her room and locked the door.

The sight of the tumbled bed inexplicably brought tears
to her eyes and she began to weep silently...perhaps for
the woman, Manara, perhaps for her daughter, Belle, who
had been deprived of her inheritance long ago...perhaps for
herself.

Gerard was not at the clinic for the next two days. He called
her, his voice polite, to say he had work in Fort Roche but
would be there on Thursday for the women's clinic. The
conversation was to the point, no words wasted. Although
Jan had wanted that, a sense of loss was her predominant
emotion as she went about her work. Well, she told herself,
this was all temporary. Soon she would be back at her

proper job. That thought did not bring her the satisfaction she'd expected.

When the day of the clinic arrived, Jan felt sick with anxiety at the coming meeting with Gerard. If only she did not find his casual insouciance so attractive, it would be easier to concentrate on work. It was doubtful that the atmosphere between them would not be obvious to Anne.

By the time Anne got there that morning Jan, who had arrived very early, had organized the tasks that she would have to perform when their patients arrived.

'Mornin', Dr Newsome,' the nurse greeted her. 'Nice to see you again.'

'Hullo, Anne, nice to see you too.' Jan smiled, looking more efficient than she felt in her clean white lab coat over a blouse and skirt, a stethoscope in the pocket. Her pale hair, a little bleached by the sun, was secured in a neat bun, and she had applied subtle make-up to her face, now the colour of pale honey. She looked attractive, in command and, she hoped, every inch a doctor. That would be her armor against Gerard de Prescy.

'I'd appreciate a quick run-down of the routine, Anne,' she said, 'before Dr Gerard arrives.'

'Well,' Anne said, 'this will be more extensive than our usual women's clinic. We're going to take cervical smears from the women, and *you* have to show *me* how to deal with the cervical cells for the human papilloma virus tests. That's a sexually transmitted virus, isn't it?'

'Yes, it's quite common, and it's instrumental in the development of cervical cancer,' Jan explained. 'If a test comes back positive the woman will have to have the test repeated. If it's positive again we would probably do a biopsy of the cervix, then later perhaps a cauterization of the superficial cells of the cervix to get rid of the abnormal layer of cells before they become invasive.'

'Yes,' Anne said, pouring herself a cup of coffee which she would drink while she worked. 'We'll have to explain to the women that the cervix is the opening into the uterus, or the womb. Most women don't have much idea of their own anatomy.'

Gerard arrived at the same time as their first patient, almost as though he had timed it that way, so there was little breathing space for awkwardness. They were polite and professional, while Anne chatted in her usual way. Inwardly, Jan's emotions were in turmoil. As the clinic proceeded, whenever Jan found herself in close proximity to Gerard she found an excuse to move away if she could. Once or twice she saw Anne looking at her sharply.

The morning and early afternoon passed by quickly with no real break for lunch, only time for a quick sandwich and a drink. Women came in large numbers to have the tests, including the blood sugar and hemoglobin tests, which could be done on the spot.

Keeping the records straight and getting the lab requisition forms written and in order was very time-consuming. All the specimens, with their forms, would be packed into insulated boxes and transported to the labs at Fort Roche. Anything that could not be coped with there would be sent offshore by air to one of the other islands.

'Anne,' Gerard said, as they were finishing up the clinic, 'would you mind taking the specimens back with you to Fort Roche? You might as well go a bit early. Dr Newsome and I can clear up here. That would save me time later.'

'Certainly, Dr Gerard,' Anne said, giving him a surreptitious look. 'I'll leave in about ten minutes, if that's all right with you.'

It seemed obvious to Jan that he was manipulating things so that the two of them could be alone. He wanted to talk to her, and her heart began an accelerated beat. Feeling like a trapped animal, she racked her brains for ways and means of escape. If he were to touch her again she might not be able to keep her resolve.

'Is something going on between you and Dr Gerard?' Anne whispered to her as she prepared to leave. 'I've never seen him uptight like this before. And I've been thinking all the time how good you were for him, how he needs a woman just like you, someone who understands his work...and him. Isobel wasn't like that, by all accounts. Don't say you quarreled? I know it's none of my business, but I do have to work with you both.'

'It's all right, Anne.' Jan tried a laugh, not very successfully. Instead, she felt as though she wanted to cry, 'We haven't exactly quarreled—just a little tension about a personal matter, that's all. It will blow over.'

'I certainly hope so,' Anne whispered. 'Well...'bye. I've got to get these specimens to their destination before the ice melts.' In moments she was driving away down the hill.

'Jan, I want to talk to you.' Gerard stood in the doorway of the tiny office, blocking it. The crumpled white lab coat that he wore over his clothes accentuated his broad chest and his height, being slightly too small for him. Unconsciously, her eyes went over him. When he crossed the small space to reach her where she stood behind the desk she backed up against the wall.

'There isn't any more to say at the moment,' she said desperately, unnerved by the wild look on his face and her own trembling awareness of him.

'Jan...' He touched her cheek with his rough, warm hand. 'We can't work together, without clearing the air. Maybe things did move ahead too quickly. I'm sorry if that is the case. I thought it was something you wanted too. Again...I apologize if I was mistaken. We can at least be friends, can't we?'

'Don't.' Jan moved her head sideways, away from his touch. He was inches away from her and she held her breath as long as she could, pressing her body against the unyielding wall.

'It's true that I did…want to make love to you,' Jan admitted, not given to dishonesty, 'but I think it's gone far enough. I think you are trying to…to influence me that way because you want Manara.' She could have moved sideways, pushed aside the chair to walk away, but somehow it seemed so undignified.

'I wouldn't do that,' he said, 'even if I thought it was necessary.'

Eventually she had to look at him. When his head came down towards hers she stood as though hypnotized. Her lips were parting and her eyes closing for his kiss, then she moved her head. 'No… We mustn't do this…it's no good.'

Jan almost sobbed with a mixture of frustrated longing and relief when a loud banging interrupted them. Someone was hammering frantically on the outer screen door of the clinic.

Gerard was the first to get there. He met a disheveled woman coming through the door, out of breath from walking up the hill.

'Hello,' he greeted her. 'Can we help you?'

'It not me,' the woman panted. 'It my husband. He not well. Got fever.' The door swung shut behind her and she stood uneasily before them, a working woman dressed in an odd assortment of clothing.

The two doctors exchanged glances.

'Since when?' Gerard asked.

'Since the day before yesterday he not feel well,' the woman said. She was middle-aged, and looked as though she had just come from cooking. 'Then today he have pains all over, his eyes hurt him, he burning hot…not want to speak to me. He have rash too. Look like the fever to me.'

Jan looked at Gerard. 'Dengue?' she said.

'Sounds like it. The people here know what to look for.'

'Where do you live?' Jan said. 'We'll lock up here and drive there.'

'Down off the beach road,' the woman said. 'Careenage Lane.'

'We should take both cars,' Gerard said to Jan, shrugging out of his lab coat. 'One of us may have to come back here to make arrangements—to use the telephone if he has to go to hospital by ambulance. Are you ready to leave, Jan?'

'Just let me get my bag.'

'We'll be with you in a couple of minutes,' he said to the woman. 'Have a seat here, help yourself to a drink of juice or water.'

'Do you put patients in isolation when they have dengue?' Jan asked when they were back in the office. She also took off her white coat.

'No, it's not practicable in patients' homes, unfortunately, although we do give them mosquito netting,' he explained as he picked up the bags of equipment he had brought with him and waited while she gathered together her belongings to take with her. 'The ones who go to hospital are kept in isolation as far as possible.' The angst they had experienced moments before was once more in abeyance.

'How often do they have to be admitted?'

'We often admit those with the hemorrhagic variety to hospital. That type can be very serious, with internal bleeding. With the others, they're nursed at home and we make home visits. We give the family mosquito netting so that mosquitoes can't get at the infected person to spread the disease. Unfortunately, that type of mosquito bites throughout the day and not just after dusk, like some other types. Let's go.'

'Give me your name and address,' Jan said to the woman as she got together the necessary papers for taking a patient history, together with syringes and test tubes for a blood test that would confirm the diagnosis.

'Macou,' the woman said. 'He's Leroy Macou.'

Jan wrote down the name, address, age and date of birth of the patient, plus a very brief medical history and a history of the current problem. 'Do you have a telephone?' she asked.

'No.'

'Has your husband been to this clinic before as a patient? If so, I'll get out his records.'

'Yes, he been here,' Mrs Macou confirmed. 'Nothing much…just for skin trouble. And one day he cut his arm with a machete. Dr Gerard sew it up.'

It took them only a few minutes to find the old medical chart in the files, then they locked up the clinic. Gerard took the woman with him in his car and led the way down the hill to the beach road, while Jan followed along behind in a small car that had been loaned to her the previous weekend by Don McLean for her use while she was on the island.

The lane where the Macou family lived was unpaved and rutted, leading up a short way from the beach area. The houses were poor and crude, made of wood, raised above the ground on wooden posts that served to prevent water getting into the living area at times of heavy rain and to keep out rats.

As Jan brought her car to a halt behind Gerard's, she looked around her with curiosity. This was the first time she had been here to what was clearly a very poor section of Eden Bay. Some of the houses were about the same size and condition as large garden sheds. Skinny dogs and semi-clothed children, most without shoes, gathered nearby as Mrs Macou led the way up a rickety flight of steps to get to one of the houses. A small brown pig rooted in the soil under the house, while a few scrawny chickens scratched in search of food beside it. The air was redolent with smoke from where householders were burning their rubbish on areas of waste ground.

The interior of the house, while very clean and orderly, was sparsely furnished in the extreme, attesting to the abject poverty of the occupants. The living quarters consisted of two rooms, a living room and a bedroom, separated by a curtain. The cooking, Jan surmised as she glanced around quickly, would be done outside in a lean-to kitchen. Such an arrangement, when the cooking was done on clay stoves that held hot charcoal, would guard against the ever-present possibility of an accidental fire that could very quickly burn down a wooden house.

When the woman pulled aside the floral curtain to allow her and Gerard to enter the bedroom, Jan could see at a glance that the occupant of the bed was seriously ill. He lay as though dead in the dim interior, flat on his back with his head turned slightly towards the wall away from them and his eyes closed. His eyes, his face, his whole body, appeared sunken, the thin, bare torso revealing prominent ribs. He wore only a pair of faded trousers. In no way did he register their presence.

Gerard, who was used to making home visits and was not usually at a loss for words, stood silently beside Jan as they stood at the foot of the bed for a few moments, staring at their patient.

Jan felt a lump of emotion rising in her throat at the pathetic material situation of this family, of the desperation that it implied. Beside their plight, her own situation seemed almost decadent. At least her father owned his house and land, while it was doubtful that these people owned much more than the clothes on their backs. Here were people who would most likely not seek medical help until things were bad.

After they had entered, two children had come into the

house to stand silently beside their mother in the doorway of the bedroom. Gerard was the first to move forward, placing his stethoscope on the man's chest to listen to his heart.

When Jan touched the man's arm, feeling for the radial pulse at the wrist, she found his skin to be burning hot. His pulse rate was rapid. Silently she took his temperature with her computerized aural thermometer. When the gadget revealed that the fever was at danger level—at the point of brain damage—she looked across at Gerard and related her findings. 'A case for the hospital?' she said quietly.

'Definitely,' he agreed, also speaking softly, not wanting to alarm the watching family any more than they already were. Then he switched on a flashlight he had brought and played the light over the man's chest to reveal a measles-like rash. 'Looks like the haemorrhagic variety.'

'Right,' Jan said, quickly going over in her mind what they had to do. The man was clearly very seriously ill. 'I'll take his blood pressure, then get an I.V. line in and give him some fluids, shall I?'

'Yes. We'll have to be careful. Watch him closely—he could be bleeding into his kidneys.'

They both began to unpack equipment.

'I'll get his wife to get some water so we can give him a tepid sponge-down, and I'll put the ice pack on his head and eyes,' he said, sorting through his equipment and placing it on the only wooden chair in the room. 'The eyes hurt a lot in this disease.'

While Jan had packed several bags of intravenous fluids, plus the sterile plastic I.V. giving-sets, Gerard had brought plenty of ice in an insulated container. At the clinic they had an electric ice-maker, which frequently proved to be extremely useful. Now both of them set to, systematically going about their business.

'Mr Macou,' Gerard said, raising his voice. 'Leroy! Leroy!'

The man's eyelids fluttered slightly, but he did not open them. Lifting one of the eyelids, Gerard shone the flashlight into the eye. The pupil contracted and the man winced, almost imperceptibly, away from the light. 'He's not in a coma, anyway,' he muttered to Jan, 'but very close to it.'

As she prepared the intravenous infusion she addressed the silent family. Fear seemed to emanate from them. 'I'm going to give him some fluid into a vein. He needs drink very badly,' she said.

'And we're going to wash him down with cool water and put some ice on his head,' Gerard added reassuringly. 'Could you possibly bring us a bowl of water, Mrs Macou?' The woman nodded.

On coming into the house, Jan had not seen a source of water. As she heard the clack-clack of Mrs Macou's sandals on the outside steps she prayed that the woman did not have to walk several hundred yards to a communal tap.

When she had the I.V. line hooked up to the bag of fluid, Jan tied the bag to the metal bedhead. With the flashlight trained on the back of her patient's hand, Jan swabbed the skin liberally with alcohol. Although there was bright sunlight outside, little light came through the one small window of the bedroom which was amply shaded by tall trees.

She tied a rubber tourniquet to her patient's forearm to make the veins stand out. With dehydration and the lowering of the blood pressure, the veins became less prominent, and it was less easy to insert the sharp angiocath into one of them. She put on a pair of rubber gloves to protect herself against hepatitis and AIDS, which were as prevalent here as they were in the outside world.

By the time the woman came back with a large metal jug full of water, and a bowl to go with it, Jan had the I.V. in and running and Gerard had withdrawn a little blood to put in the test tube for the fever test.

Together they placed ice compresses on the patient's

head, eyes, on his neck over the carotid arteries, in the armpits and over the groin area on each side where the femoral arteries passed close to the surface as they went from the pelvis into the legs. Gerard had eased off the man's trousers, the only item of clothing that he wore. In this way, if they could cool the blood in the major arteries his temperature would begin to go down.

It was important to get the temperature down a few degrees quickly, but not so quickly after that that their patient would start to shiver and go into shock. Jan checked his temperature again before she poured water into the bowl for the tepid sponge. 'Do you have electricity here?' she asked Mrs Macou.

The woman shook her head. 'No.'

'That's a pity. We could have put some fans on him and got his temperature down more quickly.' As she spoke she added some surgical alcohol to the water in the bowl to aid evaporation of the fluid from the skin, and proceeded to sponge down the man quickly, starting with his torso.

Gradually, Leroy began to show more signs that he was alive. As his temperature dropped he made a few moaning sounds and moved his head feebly from side to side, yet when Jan lifted his arm a few inches up from the bed to sponge it he let it fall listlessly as though he had no energy.

'I've never seen one as bad as this,' Gerard said quietly to Jan. 'I'll roll him over on his side so that you can sponge down his back and legs. Careful of the ice packs.'

When the sponge-down was complete, Gerard checked the vital signs again. 'That's better, much better,' he murmured with satisfaction. 'He's as stable as we can get him for now, I think.'

Leroy groaned, a pathetic sound. One of his children began to cry softly.

'Let's see if he'll take a drink by mouth,' Gerard said, and poured cool water from a bottle into a special feeding cup with a spout, and held it to the man's lips. Tentatively at first, their patient let the water into his mouth, then swallowed painfully. Gradually he took more, with noisy swallows, as though he were parched—as he undoubtedly was, Jan surmised compassionately.

'Shall I drive back to the clinic to call an ambulance while you explain to the family that we want him in the hospital for a few days?' Jan queried.

'Yes, that's all right with me. Could you bring some more ice back with you? I'll give out the mosquito netting to the family. You know where to find the telephone number for the ambulance?'

'Yes.'

During the drive back to the clinic Jan kept the vivid image of the severely ill man in her mind. Now she wondered how she could have thought that Millie Strong might have dengue fever. At the same time, it was possible that this man had another underlying chronic illness, such as tuberculosis, that contributed to his severely febrile condition. Once in the hospital he could be given a chest X-ray. She would order one.

It did not take long for her to arrange for an ambulance to come from Fort Roche or to call Don McLean's office at the hospital to say that a patient was coming in with haemorrhagic dengue fever. Then she filled the ice container with fresh ice, smeared insect repellent on her exposed skin and drove back to the Macaous'.

It had been a long, tiring day. If this was anything to go by, she told herself wearily as she parked her car, she was in for a hectic time for the remainder of her stay on the island, especially if they had an outbreak of dengue.

'We'll change the ice packs,' Gerard said to her when she got back. 'That's about all we can do here.'

It was wonderful to lie in a bath full of scented, tepid water back at Manara later that evening. With her eyes closed,

Jan mentally reviewed the day's work. Gerard had driven to Fort Roche behind the ambulance to be with Leroy Macou when he was admitted. Later he had telephoned her at Manara to say that their patient's condition was serious but improved from the time they had first seen him.

'I ordered him a chest X-ray,' Jan had reminded him.

'That will get done tomorrow. Goodnight, Jan.'

She could not get Leroy Macou out of her mind. He seemed malnourished, perhaps worn out by hard manual labour as well. Tomorrow she would call the hospital to find out the results of the full medical work-up and blood tests, if they were available that quickly, and get information about his general health. Gerard would most likely have ordered tests for parasites as well, the effects of which could be very debilitating. Some time next week she would drive in to Fort Roche to see him, and perhaps take his wife with her...if he survived that long.

CHAPTER ELEVEN

THE man with dengue fever was in a small room by himself, Jan found when she and Mrs Macou visited him the following Wednesday, having left the nurse in charge of the Eden Bay clinic. The room had tightly fitted mosquito netting over the window and the bed was draped with net screens.

Before going in, Jan identified herself to the nurse in charge and asked permission to visit him. After all, she was only a temporary doctor on the island and did not want to take liberties. The nurse handed her Mr Macou's chart.

Not surprisingly, Leroy Macou did not recognize her so she had to explain very briefly who she was, to which he merely smiled wanly and nodded. Although he was obviously still quite ill and weak, his condition had improved in that he was more alert. Intravenous fluid still dripped into a vein in the back of his hand.

'I'll be leaving to go back to Eden Bay in about an hour,' she said to Mrs Macou, who seemed shy in the hospital setting. 'I'll come back here to get you.' There was no way of knowing whether man and wife would have much to say to each other.

Out in the corridor Jan went through his chart meticulously, checking on the tests that had been done on him and noting that Gerard had ordered everything that would be relevant. A blood test had confirmed the diagnosis of dengue fever. A chest X-ray had been done, but the report was not back from the radiologist. Neither were the results there from the tests for blood and intestinal parasites—those would take time.

After returning the chart to the nurse, Jan went to the X-ray department to see if she could get the report. Once again she introduced herself to the staff there, who obligingly went to look for the report and to find the radiologist.

'Hullo, Dr Newsome. So pleased to meet you. I'm Dr Ramaransingh, the radiologist. Yes, we did take an X-ray of your patient.' They shook hands formally. He was an East Indian man, middle-aged, with a Trinidadian accent and a very warm smile. 'Now…let me see.' He riffled through a sheaf of reports in his hands. 'Yes…here we are. It was as you suspected, Dr Newsome. He has, I'm very much afraid, a touch of the tuberculosis. Just a touch, you understand…quite treatable…in the early stages. I can show you the pictures if you would like to see them.'

'I think I would, please, if I'm not taking up too much of your time.'

Within a few minutes they were looking at the X-ray plates which had been put up on a lighted display box in a semi-darkened room. There were frontal and lateral views of the man's lungs.

'See here.' Dr Ramaransingh touched a spot on the X-ray with the tip of a pencil. 'This area in the right lower lobe…this is indicative of tuberculosis. Not too bad. As soon as he is well over the dengue fever we will start him on the tuberculosis drugs…keep him here for a while.'

'Could this be a cancer?' Jan asked, having had cancer on her mind.

'No, it is not a cancer,' the radiologist said decisively, 'and I know that he does not smoke.'

Things seemed to be falling into place professionally, Jan told herself with a certain satisfaction as she walked briskly away from the X-ray department. People were getting to know her, to like her, and she them. Her city life was beginning to take on a certain unreality. The more civilized pace here was very appealing. She would be sorry when it

came to an end. If only her personal affairs could get themselves sorted out...

Next, she went to Dr McLean's office, having telephoned
that morning to see if the report on her father's stomach
biopsy was back from the pathologist on one of the other
islands.

"Morning, Dr Newsome,' a secretary greeted her. 'Dr
McLean's in the operating theatres now. He said you would
be here to look at the report.' The young woman smiled,
and handed her an envelope. Don McLean had told her that
the tissue from the stomach showed no sign of cancer, just
evidence of inflammatory disease, so her perusal of the report was just a formality.

'Thanks.' Jan handed the report back. 'That's a relief.'
Later she would telephone her father with the news.

When she left the hospital with Mrs Macou she felt an
irrational disappointment that she had not seen Gerard.

Back at the clinic, she called her father at Manara.

'That's wonderful,' he said, when she told him about the
report. 'Tomorrow morning we'll make another phone call
to your mother and give her the news. I think it's about
time we did that, don't you?'

'Definitely.' Jan laughed. 'I think she's planning to come
out for a visit while she's got both of us in one place.'

'Yes, I got that impression too.'

The following week was hectic. Gerard came twice to help
her, as well as the nurse. There was little time for conversation about anything other than work. On both occasions
Gerard was on call for the hospital in the evenings so he
departed as soon as they finished work. Any comments of
a personal nature revolved around her father's health. The
tension was there, unmistakable, between them.

'You know,' Anne said thoughtfully at the end of one
day, when they were taking a very welcome tea-break, 'Dr

Gerard's wife never wanted children. He told me that once. She worked for the hotel chain that her family owned and she was very much a career-woman, a real extrovert too, She loved to party, so I heard.'

'Just as well they didn't have any children,' Jan commented, keeping her tone neutral, by now well attuned to nuances in the nurse's observations.

'Ah, but he wanted them,' Anne said. 'He's so good with kids, obviously likes them.'

'Mmm,' Jan murmured, knowing that Anne was leading up to something.

'He did say once that he doubted he'd ever marry again. I'm not surprised, really, because Isobel wasn't suited to be a doctor's wife.' Anne looked at her sideways. 'It's such a pity. He's a lovely man, and I know he does want children. I bet he would change his mind if the right woman came along.'

Over the past week Anne had been telling her a lot about Gerard, the information quite unasked-for. The tension must be getting to her too, Jan guessed. Perhaps the nurse suspected that they had become lovers, then sensed the strain they both experienced from having called a halt.

'Mmm,' Jan said again, as she sorted papers on the office desk. Biting her lip hard and bending her head, she felt tears form in her eyes. 'Must get back to work. I want to go home on time.'

Twice during the week she drove Leroy Macou's wife to the hospital in Fort Roche to see her husband as the woman could not afford the bus fare to get there herself. It was gratifying to see that the man was improving. Even though there was no specific cure for dengue fever, he was being rehydrated and given paracetamol to control the high temperatures. Jan had broken the news to the wife that her husband had tuberculosis and had to have prolonged drug therapy.

On the Friday evening Jan was so tired that she ate supper, had a shower and went to bed early. When darkness descended at half past six in the evening it was easy to retire early for the night.

'Jan…Jan, are you awake?' Jack Newsome stood in the open doorway of his daughter's bedroom, having put on the light, his face deathly pale.

'What is it, Dad?' Jan was instantly awake, swinging her legs over the edge of her bed, as she had done so many times before when on call for the night at the hospital in Boston. 'What's the time?' Although still fuzzy with sleep, she was immediately aware that something was very wrong.

'About two o'clock. It's my ulcer, I think, playing up again.' In spite of his apparent calm, he could not keep the fear out of his voice and was obviously in pain.

'Lie down here on my bed, Dad. Quickly.' Automatically she pulled on her thin cotton robe, then fumbled hurriedly in her medical bag, which she had left on the floor, while her father lay down. Fear tensed her muscles, yet clarified her thoughts. 'Let me take your blood pressure.'

With her heart pounding—trying not to increase his anxiety by letting her fear show—she put her fingers on his pulse, then took his blood pressure. The pulse was more rapid than it should have been, the blood pressure lower.

'Just stay lying there, Dad. Keep your head down.' She put her equipment back into the bag. 'I'm going to call the hospital to say you're coming in. It's better to go there because you may be bleeding a bit.'

Jan's thoughts jumped rapidly from one possibility to another. It was not uncommon for a stomach ulcer to bleed or to perforate. In the latter event the stomach contents leaked into the peritoneal cavity, causing life-threatening peritonitis as well as the immediate possibility of a quick death from a massive haemorrhage.

Jack Newsome nodded, closing his eyes. There were small beads of sweat on his upper lip and on his forehead.

Using the telephone in the sitting room, Jan dialled the hospital number. It was doubtful that her father had a perforation of the stomach—he would be in more pain and in shock. It was possible, though, that she could have a perforation on her hands *en route* to the hospital. Better get an ambulance.

As she listened to the ringing tone she pressed her fingers against her eyelids, eyes that felt dry from lack of adequate sleep. This was the very scenario for which she had come to St Bonar, either to prevent or to deal with. It was all happening like a scene from a play that she had to perform, whether she wanted to or not. Vaguely she felt thankful that tomorrow was not a working day for her. 'Hurry! Hurry…please.'

'Royal Hospital.' A man's voice responded at last

Hastily, the words tripping over themselves, Jan explained what was happening. 'Could you contact Dr Don McLean, please?' she asked the switchboard operator, her voice trembling. 'I think he's the one on call for surgery.'

'Do you want an ambulance?' the man queried.

'Well, I would like one but we can't wait here at the house—I think it's too urgent.' She kept her voice low. 'Could we rendezvous with the ambulance on the road? Then they could take over. I'll be driving a Land Rover.' There was only one road to Fort Roche so there was no possibility that they could miss each other.

'Yes. We'll be on our way as fast as we can.'

It was all settled. Jan ran back to her room, pulled on jeans and a blouse, grabbed her medical kit and handbag then went to her father's room to get pillows and blankets from his bed.

The telephone rang as she was about to go outside.

'Hello, Jan.' It was the comforting voice of Don McLean. 'It sounds as though you've got a bit of trouble there.'

'Yes, I'm afraid so, Dr McLean,' Jan said, knowing that her voice was uneven with fear. She enlarged upon what she had told the hospital operator.

'It certainly sounds like a bit of a bleed,' he said. 'I'm surprised about that. I thought he would be healing up nicely by now. If we have to operate, Jan, I'll get Gerard to help me. He's not on call with me tonight but I'll get him.'

'Yes...please. I'd like it to be him.' Surprisingly, perhaps, Jan knew that she meant it...fervently. The knowledge was a revelation of sorts, although there was no time to dwell on it.

'Now, don't you worry too much. Keep him lying down and get him here as fast as you can.'

'Yes, I will. Thank you.'

Running down the front steps, her slim figure dwarfed by the pile of bedding she was carrying, Jan prayed that Gerard would be available. Sometimes, she knew, he went out on his boat, a yacht, at weekends. She had a vision of Gerard on that boat, docked somewhere, perhaps off a tiny, uninhabited island. Perhaps he would have a woman with him.

Desperately she tried to push that thought from her mind. Over the past weeks on St Bonar she had come to trust the man with the rough, working-man's hands...even though he both disturbed and attracted her beyond her usual ability to cope with ease.

When she had made up a comfortable place for her father to lie down in the back of the Land Rover, which she had parked by the front steps, she led him carefully out of the house, thankful that he could still walk. 'Steady, Dad, take it easy. You'll be all right.'

When he was settled she took off, and went as fast as

she dared, knowing that this was life or death for her father. Once on the paved road she picked up speed, driving with a skill and concentration she hadn't known she possessed. She took the sharp bends closely, racing along open stretches. The clock on the dashboard told her that it was half past two. Small villages were closed and silent. There was no other traffic on the road.

About halfway to Fort Roche, in an open area of banana plantation, she saw the ambulance tearing towards her, its red emergency light flickering on top. Jan slowed down, clicking her headlights on and off to alert them, then pulled over at the side of the road.

The ambulance came to a halt with a dramatic squeal of tires. Fortunately, there were no other vehicles on the road.

'Dr Newsome?' The two attendants got out.

'Yes.'

With commendable speed and efficiency, Jack was transferred by stretcher to the more comfortable ambulance.

'I'll follow on behind, Dad. See you at the hospital. Don't worry too much now…everything's under control.' Her lips trembled as she kissed his clammy forehead, hoping that she sounded more confident than she felt. Before letting him go, she felt his pulse again. Not too bad…but not good either.

'Be as quick as you can,' she whispered to the driver as he climbed back in. 'He's bleeding…probably quite badly.'

'Don't you worry, darling, ' the driver whispered back, squeezing her arm reassuringly. 'We give him some oxygen and some I.V. fluids. Dr McLean and Dr Gerard are waiting there for him in the casualty department. We get him there like greased lightning.'

'Thank you.'

After turning round, the ambulance raced back down the dark road the way it had come, and quickly disappeared from view.

Only then did Jan's spurious calm desert her. She stood in the road and wept. 'Please, God, keep him safe,' she whispered over and over again.

Her father would be better off in the ambulance. They had the necessary equipment to keep him going, and the driver knew the road better than she did.

The night was very quiet, very dark. The headlights of the Land Rover lit up the dense vegetation on either side of the road, making her feel vulnerable and alone. There was the question now of how soon she should contact her mother and brother in England to let them know. In any event, she would have to wait until after the operation.

She climbed back into the driver's seat to finish the journey, knowing that by the time she got to the Royal Hospital they would probably have started to operate on her father.

CHAPTER TWELVE

THE doctors' lounge, next to the operating theatres, was a small, cluttered room where surgeons and anesthetists rested briefly between operations. It contained a few utilitarian plastic-covered sofas and chairs. A coffee-table was littered with yesterday's newspapers and a few old medical journals. In the early hours of the morning the place was quiet.

It was here that Jan sat, the only occupant, a cup of cooling coffee in her hand from which she forced herself to sip from time to time. She was oblivious to her surroundings, only vaguely aware of their sparse comfort and the cloying heat in the enclosed space, when the ache in her heart dominated her being. It was a place where sober thoughts came naturally.

The operation had been going on for some time. The hands on her wrist-watch seemed to be scarcely moving. Surely any minute now someone would be out to speak to her.

Dr McLean was the first to come in, waving at her to remain seated when she struggled tiredly to her feet, her face taut with worry. He flopped down in a chair opposite her.

'Ah... That's better,' he said, pulling off his face mask and green cotton operating cap. 'I'm getting a bit old for this night lark, Jan. Let me put you out of your misery. Gerard's just finishing for me in there, doing the sewing-up. He's a great surgeon.' He wiped sweat from his forehead with a large piece of surgical gauze that he pulled from his pocket. 'Your dad's all right now.'

'Thank God for that.' Tears stung her eyes as she looked down at her hands which were tightly clasped.

'Here, take this,' Dr McLean said gruffly, as he handed her a fresh piece of gauze. 'I always keep some of this on me for emergencies.'

'Thanks.' She managed a weak smile.

'As you've probably guessed,' he went on, 'we had to do a partial gastrectomy. He was bleeding steadily and had lost quite a bit of blood. Quite possibly he could have perforated if we'd waited any longer. I took out as little of the stomach as I could get away with. He should be fine after this if we keep him on antibiotics for a while. There shouldn't be any recurrence.'

'No...' Jan said, trying to force her mind ahead to all that they would have to do. 'I'm very grateful for what you've done, Dr McLean. In a way, I'm glad this has happened while I'm on the island. If he'd been alone the outcome might not have been so good.'

'Maybe this will force him to review his situation,' Don McLean said, looking at her shrewdly. 'I would be sorry to see Jack leave the island altogether, but sometimes you have to make a move. It's better to make a change when you know you have to rather than wait to have it thrust upon you—as he has done now.'

'Don't I know it!' Jan said feelingly, scrubbing at her face. 'He's a stubborn man.'

They continued to talk for some time, then Dr McLean got to his feet.

'Stay here, Jan. Gerard wants to talk to you. We'll keep your dad in the recovery room overnight, then we'll put him in a single room in the surgical ward. You can see him as soon as he's been transferred.'

After he had gone Jan's spirits lifted gradually. She wiped away a few stray tears with the gauze. So far so good. For a man of her father's age, the recovery period was also a time of possible problems, although he had never smoked so she assumed that his heart and lungs were in good condition. Tomorrow she would call her mother. Maybe she would come to take him back to England, leaving Manara to its fate.

'Hullo, Jan.' Suddenly Gerard was there, his presence breaking into her thoughts and dominating the scruffy little room.

It seemed natural that he would kiss her briefly on the cheek when she stood up to face him. 'Your father's all right. He's just been taken to the recovery room.' His face was serious, tired, his manner with her very gentle. 'The operation was routine for what he had. Everything went smoothly so there's no reason to suppose that he won't make a full recovery.'

'Thank you for getting up in the middle of the night when it wasn't your turn to be on call. I...I'm very grateful,' she blurted out, feeling close to tears again, oddly shy with him.

'I would have been annoyed if I hadn't been called,' he said, taking off his operating cap and running a hand through his thick, springy hair. 'Now, when you've seen your father what are you going to do for the remainder of the night? I don't think you should be alone at Manara, and there's no point in going back there now anyway. You'll want to see your father tomorrow.'

'I hadn't thought that far ahead,' she said.

'I want to invite you to stay at my house,' he said in a matter-of-fact manner, 'then you could be on hand if you were needed. I have a spare room. I'm going to stay here for a while, of course, until your father's recovered from the anaesthetic, then I'll be heading home. I suggest you come with me then.' It was more like an order than a suggestion. He was also very businesslike. It was not like an invitation from a former lover.

Jan nodded. 'Thank you,' she said. Once again he seemed to be lifting events out of her hands. Unlike the first time, when they had met on the road, she was glad and pleasantly comforted. It was a feeling she had not experienced for some time. She let herself go with it.

Later she went to the recovery room to see her father. He lay on a stretcher, looking pale and somehow shrunken, a rubber airway still in his mouth. Taking his limp hand in hers, she leaned over him so that her mouth was near his ear. 'The operation's over, Dad. Everything's all right.' To her own ears her voice sounded high, tremulous.

His eyelids came open slowly, revealing watery eyes that were blank with incomprehension. Using a piece of gauze, Jan carefully wiped his eyes and repeated her message several times until she saw some light of understanding in him.

Gerard came to stand beside her to look at the electronic monitors that were recording her father's vital signs. Gerard's face was taut with concentration, his lips compressed into a serious line. Like her, he looked as though he could use several days of sleep.

'I would like to stay until he's fully aware of what has happened,' Jan said to Gerard, her voice breaking. 'So...so that he knows I'm here, that I haven't deserted him.'

'Of course,' Gerard said, his dark eyes narrowed as he scrutinized her features, which she knew were vulnerable with emotion. 'There are things I have to do here too. We'll leave together. First, we need a break. Come outside, give the nurses a chance to do their thing.'

Unprotestingly, she allowed him to take her by the elbow and lead her out of the room. 'I'll be at Frank's,' he said to one of the nurses as they left.

Jan did not say a word as, still holding her arm, he walked with her out of the hospital into the velvety, dark warmth of the tropical night.

'There's a little all-night café across the street,' Gerard

said, by way of explanation. 'Frank's. I think we both need something to eat.'

The café was little more than a hole in the wall, from which tantalizing smells of spicy cooking emanated. Several of the hospital lab staff were there, squeezed into the small space where customers sat on tall stools at counters fixed to the walls. No one turned a hair when Gerard appeared in his green scrub suit.

'Hello, Dr Gerard,' one of them called, smiling a welcome. 'Business as usual, eh?'

'What you have, Dr Gerard?' the woman behind the counter called.

'Two beers, Lucretia,' he said, 'and two of those great vegetarian rotis you make. Then we'll have two chunks of the coconut pie, please.'

Gerard squeezed into a corner space, maneuvering Jan ahead of him so that they were both perched on stools. 'I'm starved,' he said. 'Hypoglycemic.' Deftly he removed the tops from the two bottles of ice-cold beer as they were passed to him via a human chain.

'Gerard, I...I don't think I could eat anything,' Jan began, aware of a sick feeling of anxiety still in the pit of her stomach, even though she needed a source of energy.

'Force yourself,' Gerard said crisply, concentrating on pouring the beer into glasses. 'That's an order. You'll feel better for it. I have my bleeper in my pocket.' He indicated the electronic gadget clipped to the pocket of his surgical pants. 'They'll page me if there's anything we need to know. We can be back over there in sixty seconds.'

Jan bit her lip, looking down at the glass of golden beer.

She realized that she had missed him—missed the closeness, his uncalculated pleasure in her. It seemed obvious now that his desire to own Manara had nothing to do with it. Most of all she missed the joy he had given her...for she could see now that that was what it had been.

An insight came to her then, sharp and sobering in its clarity, that she had not wanted to get into something with him that would not be permanent. That was why she had drawn back— because he was the sort of man with whom one should be with permanently. Would want to be...

'Drink,' he said.

The beer was imbibed in short order, inducing a mild sense of relaxation that she so badly needed. The hot rotis, thin folded pastry envelopes stuffed with spicy vegetables, were delicious. As Jan bit into one she found that she was hungry after all. Gradually, something of the awful tension in her began to subside.

'This is the only café in the whole of Fort Roche where you can get a really superb cup of coffee,' Gerard confided, when he had ordered coffee to go with the thick wedges of coconut pie. The pie was made from shredded coconut mixed with condensed milk and baked in a pastry shell.

'You've come to my rescue, haven't you...once again?' she said. 'You must think I'm a woman who needs to be rescued. Anyway, Gerard, thank you...for being in the right place at the right time. Thank you for everything.'

When his face darkened Jan realized that he had flushed with pleasure at her thanks. Intuitively, she knew that he had not received a personal compliment for quite some time...perhaps because he had not allowed it.

Now she felt an acknowledgement crackle between them. Anne's words came back to her.

'What are you smiling at?' he said.

'I was thinking of something that Anne said. She thinks you're a lovely man.'

He threw back his head and laughed, the gesture erasing the tiredness on his face.

My God! I love him...I love him. As though she had spoken aloud, those words were spelled out in her mind as she stared at his eyes which were warm with amusement.

'And do you think that?' he queried softly.

'Yes...yes, I do.'

Silently they finished their coffee, each immersed in private thoughts yet united in their consciousness of each other.

While Gerard paid for their meal Jan left a generous tip under her saucer. Anxious now to get back to her father, there was no time to analyze her troubled thoughts regarding Gerard.

'Feeling better now?' he said, as they left.

Not trusting her voice, Jan nodded and smiled.

There was a small unlit garden, filled with palms of different types, that they had to traverse to get to the street. As they picked their way through it Jan was very aware of Gerard's nearness so that when his bare arm accidentally brushed against hers she drew in her breath sharply. In an instant Gerard had pulled her effortlessly into his arms, holding her against his powerful body.

'Jan.' He whispered her name.

In the black shadow of a tree he kissed her, his mouth crushing hers hungrily. She did not pull away. As she parted her lips to receive him she knew that this was what she wanted, what she had been waiting for ever since the last time he had touched her. With a small cry of surrender she put her arms up around his neck.

Three quarters of an hour had gone by before they were back in the hospital to see Jack Newsome once again. With expert efficiency Gerard checked his vital signs while Jan stood wondering whether the nurses had any hint that a few moments ago she and Gerard had been in the throes of a helpless passion that had left her emotionally shattered.

Surreptitiously she looked at him. At the moment he gave no hint of how his calm had deserted him as he had strained her against him as though he wanted to incorporate her into his own body—no hint of her fevered reciprocation. Only her flushed cheeks, perhaps, gave her away.

'Everything is as it should be,' he commented to Jan as she stood on the other side of the stretcher. 'I'm going to get changed now. I'll come back here for you.'

Jan nodded. Looking down at her father, whose eyes were closed, she could see a difference in him already. His color had improved and his breathing was regular. He was now sleeping a more natural sleep. Not wanting to wake him, she simply stood looking at him, a silent exemplar of the love of a child for its parent.

Standing there, feeling almost like a child in her crumpled jeans and thin blouse, a new insight came to her—paradoxically, of how much she had grown up since her arrival on the island, as though she had been forced to a new stage of maturity in a hurry.

Listening to her father's quiet breathing in the hushed room, Jan knew there would be some changes in her life.

'Ready?' Gerard was back, dressed in light outdoor clothing, carrying his medical bag.

'Yes,' she said.

CHAPTER THIRTEEN

'GOODNIGHT, Jan,' Gerard said, at the door of a guest bedroom in his breezy house near the top of a hill in Fort Roche. 'What's left of it. We'll talk tomorrow.'

'Yes. Goodnight.'

They were both so exhausted that they slept. In the morning they went to see her father and found that he had been transferred to a single room in a general surgical ward. He was alert and talkative, mildly sedated for pain, his color much improved from the pale, sickly hue of the day before.

'Jan, talk to Gerard about the estate,' he said urgently, weakly. 'I'm not going to have the energy for some time.'

Picking up his hand, Jan squeezed it gently. 'It's all right, Dad, I'll take care of everything. Yes, I will talk to him.'

'And your mother,' he said. 'Tell her to come if she can.'

'It's all organized, Dad. She wants to come.'

The effort of talking tired him and he closed his eyes, drifting into sleep.

Gerard arranged free time and drove behind her to Manara. They had agreed to talk and he would stay there with her for a few days. Already the house seemed to have changed when Jan unlocked the heavy mahogany front door. It seemed to be waiting, as though for a new owner. Maybe it's just me, Jan told herself sadly, entering the hallway, knowing that my father isn't here.

'You've won in a way, haven't you, Gerard?' she said, turning to him. 'You want this house... We may just have to let you have it.'

'You think so?' he said softly as he followed her to the kitchen to get a drink.

The kitchen was cool and dim, its window and door, opening to a side verandah, shaded by tall trees. As Jan went to the refrigerator to get out a jug of fruit juice and to find glasses for them, she was aware of the familiar swift tension between her and Gerard. She wished that he would not stand quietly, watching her with that unsmiling intensity.

Their fingers touched as she handed him a full glass of fruit juice, heightening her awareness of him and her own sudden inability to think of anything to say. Indeed, her throat seemed to have closed up so that she could not have uttered a word. Last night concern for her father had wiped everything else from her mind. Now, knowing that he was all right, other considerations were allowed a place.

Grabbing her own glass, she skirted Gerard to go out to the verandah, where drinking the cool liquid restored some of her composure. Out on the lawn two purple-brown doves pecked calmly among the blades of grass and fallen blossom. Jan focused her eyes on them, aware that Gerard had come to lean against the frame of the open door. She looked at him and met his eyes quickly, then looked away again. There were unspoken questions in his stance—he was waiting for her to be ready.

I love him. Again the certainty was echoed in her brain. By comparison, her feelings for John had been juvenile, she could see that now. Instinctively, she knew that this was real, serious, uncontrollable.

Jan closed her eyes briefly, blotting out the bright morning. Was it possible that Gerard loved her? That he desired her was beyond dispute.

Taking a deep breath and then letting it out, she turned to face him. 'My father wants me to talk to you about the estate,' she said. 'If you still definitely want to buy it, he...and I...would consider selling.' Her voice shook as she said the words. 'My mother and brother have also come around to the idea.'

Patterns of shadow and sunlight played over them as he still lounged in the doorway, as though perfectly at ease. Warm air wafted over them across the verandah, which was furnished with old, comfortable rattan chairs. Jan looked around her. This was a home, not just a house—any old house.

'There is another way, Jan,' he said softly.

'What?'

'I would like to pay your father for the house.' He straightened and came towards her, putting the glass on a small table. 'Then I would like to marry you. That way I would own the house, and it would stay in your family at the same time.'

His words were like a bombshell between them. Jan felt her heart skip a beat, her cheeks flush. 'You...you would do that to get a house?'

He came to her, putting his hands on her shoulders so that she was forced to tilt her head to look up at him. Is this really happening? she asked herself, as though in a haze of unreality, when moments before she had admitted to herself again that she loved him. It was as though he had read her mind perfectly, known her need...

'I would get you,' he said. 'It's you I want. I thought I would never want to marry again, Jan, but from the time I first saw you, with your hair all messed up, driving that van, I knew that I could change my mind.'

'Why?' she whispered, as he moved his arms down to hold her in a loose embrace.

'Because I love you...with all my heart, with all my soul,' he said quietly, his face serious as he looked down at her. 'There's something about this place...as though the spirits of Manara and Henri Daviot were here, urging us to live life to the full while we're able to do so. Don't you feel it?'

'Yes...'

'There's a sense of urgency,' he said insistently. 'You're right for me, Jan, and I think I'm right for you. I know it's asking a lot for you to give up your other life to live here on St Bonar.'

'But I love it.' She breathed the words on a wave of joy, sharing his mood of slowly building elation. 'I...love you, Gerard.'

With a laugh of pure joy he picked her up, his arms under her hips to lift her high so that she was looking down on him. Tilting his face up to hers, he held her prisoner in his arms.

'Say it again, Jan,' he demanded, smiling. 'Say it.'

'I love you,' she whispered. 'So much.'

He let her slide down the length of his body, then stood, rocking her in his arms, while she put her arms around him tightly. A happiness that she had never felt before came over her like a warm flood, enveloping her totally.

'Will you marry me, then?' he said.

'Oh, yes...yes.'

'When you telephone your mother,' he said, his voice light with a new happiness, 'tell her that she could soon be a grandmother.'

'Oh, could she?' Jan pulled back to look at him.

'If I have anything to do with it, she could be.' He laughed. 'Is that what you want, Jan—for us, for Manara?'

'Yes.' As she said the word Jan knew that it was true, that she longed for children...Gerard's children. 'Very much so. There's only one condition, though.'

He stroked her hair. 'What's that?'

'That we start the process very soon,' she said laughing.

The breeze stirred the palm trees in the garden, and seemed to whisper of past love, past happiness.

'I have always maintained,' he said huskily, 'that one must seize the moment.'

'I completely agree,' she said, her heart beginning that deep accelerated beat.

'You once told me,' he said lazily, holding her against him, 'Henri Daviot's epitaph. I've forgotten it...'

'*"Paix et immortalité; joie; amour; et Manara"*.' She quoted the words softly.

'"Peace and immortality...joy...love...and Manara",' he translated, his deep voice, as he said the familiar words, sending a frisson of understanding through Jan, as though a voice from the past had spoken to her. This love, this promise, was the most important thing in life.

'Yes... That's it...precisely,' he added.

'Gerard...' Jan whispered his name.

'Come,' he said.

They went into the quiet sitting room. With a singleness of purpose they lay down side by side on the horsehair sofa. 'This must have been made for us,' he murmured as she reached for him and he gathered her to him. She felt safe, enclosed. The present, past and future were in her arms.

In the garden the mourning doves began to call. This time their message was of hope, welcome, love...

MILLS & BOON®

Makes any time special

**Enjoy a romantic novel from
Mills & Boon®**

Presents™ *Enchanted*™ *Temptation*.

Historical Romance™ *Medical Romance*™

MILLS & BOON®

Next Month's Romance Titles

♡

Each month you can choose from a wide variety of romance novels from Mills & Boon®. Below are the new titles to look out for next month from the Presents™ and Enchanted™ series.

Presents™

THE PERFECT LOVER	Penny Jordan
TO BE A HUSBAND	Carole Mortimer
THE BOSS'S BABY	Miranda Lee
ONE BRIDEGROOM REQUIRED!	Sharon Kendrick
THE SEXIEST MAN ALIVE	Sandra Marton
FORGOTTEN ENGAGEMENT	Margaret Mayo
A RELUCTANT WIFE	Cathy Williams
THE WEDDING BETRAYAL	Elizabeth Power

Enchanted™

THE MIRACLE WIFE	Day Leclaire
TEXAS TWO-STEP	Debbie Macomber
TEMPORARY FATHER	Barbara McMahon
BACHELOR AVAILABLE!	Ruth Jean Dale
BOARDROOM BRIDEGROOM	Renee Roszel
THE HUSBAND DILEMMA	Elizabeth Duke
THE BACHELOR BID	Kate Denton
THE WEDDING DECEPTION	Carolyn Greene

On sale from 5th February 1999

H1 9901

ELIZABETH GAGE

When Dusty brings home her young fiancé, he
is everything her mother Rebecca Lowell could
wish for her daughter, *and for herself...*

The Lowell family's descent into darkness
begins with one bold act, one sin
committed in an otherwise blameless life.
This time there's no absolution in...

Confession

AVAILABLE FROM JANUARY 1999

He's a cop, she's his prime suspect

MARY LYNN BAXTER

HARD CANDY

He's crossed the line no cop ever should.
He's involved with a suspect—his
prime suspect.

Falling for the wrong man is far down her
list of troubles.

Until he arrests her for murder.

2FREE
books and a surprise gift!

We would like to take this opportunity to thank you for reading this Mills & Boon® book by offering you the chance to take TWO more specially selected titles from the Medical Romance™ series absolutely FREE! We're also making this offer to introduce you to the benefits of the Reader Service™—

> ★ FREE home delivery
> ★ FREE gifts and competitions
> ★ FREE monthly Newsletter
> ★ Books available before they're in the shops
> ★ Exclusive Reader Service discounts

Accepting these FREE books and gift places you under no obligation to buy, you may cancel at any time, even after receiving your free shipment. Simply complete your details below and return the entire page to the address below. *You don't even need a stamp!*

YES! Please send me 2 free Medical Romance books and a surprise gift. I understand that unless you hear from me, I will receive 4 superb new titles every month for just £2.30 each, postage and packing free. I am under no obligation to purchase any books and may cancel my subscription at any time. The free books and gift will be mine to keep in any case.

M9EA

Ms/Mrs/Miss/Mr..............................Initials ....
                                                                                                                BLOCK CAPITALS PLEASE
Surname ....
Address ....
....
....Postcode..........................

Send this whole page to:
THE READER SERVICE, FREEPOST CN81, CROYDON, CR9 3WZ
(Eire readers please send coupon to: P.O. BOX 4546, DUBLIN 24.)

Offer not valid to current Reader Service subscribers to this series. We reserve the right to refuse an application and applicants must be aged 18 years or over. Only one application per household. Terms and prices subject to change without notice. Offer expires 31st July 1999. As a result of this application, you may receive further offers from Harlequin Mills & Boon and other carefully selected companies. If you would prefer not to share in this opportunity please write to The Data Manager at the address above.

Medical Romance is being used as a trademark.

JoAnn
ROSS

a woman's heart

In *A Woman's Heart*, JoAnn Ross has created a
rich, lyrical love story about land, community,
family and the very special bond between a man
who doesn't believe in anything and a woman
who believes in him.

MIRA®   **Available from February**